D0965440

LOSING
THE
FIELD

Also by Abbi Glines

The Field Party Series
Until Friday Night
Under the Lights
After the Game

LOSING THE FIELD

A Field Party Novel

BY

ABBI GLINES

Simon Pulse

NEW YORK   LONDON   TORONTO   SYDNEY   NEW DELHI

SIMON PULSE
An imprint of Simon & Schuster Children's Publishing Division
1230 Avenue of the Americas, New York, New York 10020
First Simon Pulse hardcover edition August 2018
Text copyright © 2018 by Abbi Glines
Jacket photo-illustration copyright © 2018 by We Monsters
All rights reserved, including the right of reproduction
in whole or in part in any form.
SIMON PULSE and colophon are registered trademarks
of Simon & Schuster, Inc.
For information about special discounts for bulk purchases, please
contact Simon & Schuster Special Sales at 1-866-506-1949 or
business@simonandschuster.com.
The Simon & Schuster Speakers Bureau can bring authors to your live
event. For more information or to book an event contact the
Simon & Schuster Speakers Bureau at 1-866-248-3049
or visit our website at www.simonspeakers.com.
Jacket designed by Jessica Handelman
Interior designed by Mike Rosamilia
The text of this book was set in Stempel Garamond LT.
Manufactured in the United States of America
2 4 6 8 10 9 7 5 3 1
Library of Congress Cataloging-in-Publication Data
Names: Glines, Abbi, author.
Title: Losing the field / by Abbi Glines.
Description: First Simon Pulse hardcover edition. |
New York : Simon Pulse, 2018. | Series: Field party |
Summary: Seventeen-year-old Tallulah Liddell and her longtime
crush, Nash Lee, struggle through the summer to overcome emotional
wounds—she, overweight, insecure, and angry at being ridiculed by
Nash and he, the football star who survives an accident that leaves him
lost and bitter—but in spite of their pain, or perhaps because of it,
they unexpectedly find themselves falling for each other.
Identifiers: LCCN 2017057189 | ISBN 9781534403895 (hardcover) |
Subjects: | CYAC: Emotional problems—Fiction. |
Overweight persons—Fiction. | Love—Fiction. |
High schools—Fiction. | Schools—Fiction.
Classification: LCC PZ7.G4888 Lo 2018 | DDC [Fic]—dc23
LC record available at https://lccn.loc.gov/2017057189
ISBN 9781534403918 (eBook)

To the reader who has been hurt by words.
You are not defined by anyone but yourself. No words
can take away your happiness except you.
Love yourself and others will too.

To the reader who has lost a dream.
Life often changes courses, and you can choose to give
up or find a new path with an even brighter future.

LOSING
THE
FIELD

PROLOGUE

It all started in first grade. Those crystal-clear blue eyes and dimpled smile on the prettiest color skin I had ever seen. Nash Lee was the only kid who smiled at me on my first day of school. A few had snickered when I walked in. My stomach ached, and I wanted to go home. I knew it was a bad idea to wear the shorts that my momma had bought me. My thighs rubbed together when I walked, and the shorts crawled up between them, showing even more of my dimply white legs.

But Nash Lee hadn't called me "fatty" or "four eyes." When the girls had giggled when I tripped walking to the teacher's desk to sharpen my pencils, Nash had told them to stop. When the teacher mispronounced my name every day the entire first month, everyone laughed but Nash. He began correcting the teacher when I had given up after three days in a row. I would soon learn that the fat, shy girl wasn't popular with teachers, either. They made comments about the lunches I brought, and one told me to wear bigger shorts.

In my mind Nash Lee was my hero. He was kind yet popular, beautiful, and a star on the football field. He had been approached by college recruiters already. Or that's what the rumor was. I was sure there would never be a more perfect man in this world. Until the last day of our junior year. It all changed.

Tomorrow was the day I looked forward to all school year long. Like most of my classmates. However, my reasons were different. I didn't want to escape from homework and tests. I enjoyed learning. I liked to read. I had spent hours reading the websites of over fifty colleges I might want to attend. But I hated the way high school made me feel. I was ignored unless someone was using me to get some laughs from their friends.

When the school play tryouts came around, I always memorized the lines, practiced in a mirror for hours, recorded myself, and watched it to perfect anything wrong. But no matter how good I was, I never got the part. I didn't fit. I wasn't what they wanted onstage.

I was fat. I accepted it. And instead of dieting, I would go home and eat a box of cookies to make myself feel better. It was comfort to me. It didn't make fun of me. Food was where I found happiness. That and reading. I read all the time. I read so much that I reviewed books online. I had a blog that covered everything from fantasy to romance to horror. I liked it all.

In my head I was already at home reading a book, enjoying the swing on our back porch. Alone and safe from the cruelty that surrounded me. I cleaned out my locker, happy that next year I would be a senior and for sure get the top locker that I had requested the past two years and not received. With my backpack full of the items that had collected over the past nine months, I headed for the exit, so glad it would be twelve weeks before I had to walk back in those doors.

Before I could get to the door, Nash Lee and his cousin Ryker came walking inside. They were smiling and laughing. Happy with life. I wondered what that felt like. Having it all. Being loved, accepted, wanted.

"You out of here, Tallulah?" he asked, still smiling.

No one ever spoke to me or called me by my name. No one except Nash. Last year my best friend Annamae moved to Georgia. Since then I was a loner. I wasn't good at being social and making new friends.

"Yes," I replied, feeling my cheeks heat up like they always did when he spoke to me.

"Enjoy your summer. We're finally seniors!" He said the last bit with more enthusiasm. I was sure he had a big college interested in him, and he'd go get everything he had dreamed of.

"You too." Those were silly words really. As if Nash Lee wouldn't have the best summer of his life. I was sure every summer was amazing for him. He'd have parties and friends. He'd go to the beach and not be embarrassed to wear swim trunks. I hadn't worn a bathing suit and gone swimming since I was seven and someone called me "Fatty Patty" while I was at the local pool.

I did not stand there and make him keep talking to me. I figured he was kind enough to speak to me, and so I responded and went on my way. I walked past them, and when I was a good distance away I heard Ryker whisper a little too loudly, "Damn, I hope she don't wear swimsuits in the summer. No one needs to see that." Ryker then laughed as if he'd said something hilarious.

I waited for Nash to scold him. To tell him that wasn't nice. To be my hero.

Instead . . . the worst sound in the world . . . the one thing I never expected. Nash laughed too. Then they were gone inside those doors, and their laughter with them.

However, it would haunt me. It would remind me that I had no one but my mom who loved or wanted me. Not even my father had stuck around.

I had been craving my home and security all day, but when I got into my white Honda Civic, I didn't go home. Instead, I drove to the walking track at the local park, got out, and walked until I couldn't take another step. My shirt was wet with sweat. My feet ached so bad I wasn't sure I'd make it back to my car. My face was streaked with tears. But the next day I did it again. And again. And again.

I Doubt You Notice Fat Girls
CHAPTER 1

TALLULAH

"Is she new?" I heard whispered yet again as I walked into the doors of Lawton High School. I'd heard that question as I passed at least three other groups of students. People I'd gone to school with since preschool. I had often wondered if some of them even knew my name. They never spoke to me. Hardly acknowledged me.

I had blamed them for so long. However, over the summer I'd come to realize a lot of things. One being I was the one who tried to be invisible. I was shy. I didn't want attention drawn to me. Often when I did get attention it was hurtful, and I kept to the shadows as much as possible. So if they didn't know my name, then it was because I had done nothing notable. Nothing to look back on one day and be proud of.

This year would be different. I wasn't hiding now. I was tired of being the butt of everyone's jokes. I would make my senior year one to remember. One to be proud of. I was even going to join . . . something. Maybe the yearbook staff or possibly try out for the dance team. I could dance. That was my little secret. When I had weighed more than society thought I should, I hadn't wanted to dance in front of anyone. It was something I did alone.

"Hey, new girl!" a male voice called out. Since I wasn't new, I ignored him. But I did glance slightly to the left to see who it was. Asa Griffith. I almost paused. He was good friends with Ryker and Nash Lee. Ryker I didn't care about, but Nash . . . let's just say that my hurt and anger because of him were what kept me going all summer. When it was so hot I thought I'd melt, but I walked anyway. When I really wanted some hot-from-the-oven cookies, but I ate an apple instead. It had been revenge. Admitting it wasn't something that I was proud of, but it was the truth. I hated Nash Lee. But that hate had driven me to lose weight.

Before I could think too long and hard about it, I stopped and turned to Asa Griffith. He was attractive, popular, and would be the Lawton Lions star running back now that West Ashby had graduated. Asa gave me a flirty grin I had never seen before. Guys like Asa didn't smile at girls like me. Or they hadn't. I realized how shallow they were now that I was thin. My plan for revenge may be something ugly. But so was the way they treated girls due to their weight. Inside I was the same. No, that wasn't true; inside I was angrier now.

I didn't know how to flirt. I was one to shrink near a corner. So I just stared at him. Waiting to see what would come out of his mouth next.

"Asa," he said with a nod as he closed the distance between us. "You just move here?"

"No," I replied. This question I had prepared for. I was going to enjoy it. Seeing the looks on their faces when they found out they'd known me for years.

He was still smiling, but he looked confused. "Home-schooled?" he asked.

"No, Asa. We had Literature together last year. Economics the year before that. In fifth grade you tripped me in the hallway, and my books went everywhere. It was an accident. At least I assumed it was since you helped me pick up my books."

That was more fun than I realized it would be. He stood there frowning. I wondered if he even knew my name. It only fueled the fire inside me. My revenge seemed justified.

"Asa," a familiar voice called out, then a pause. I turned

my head and met his gaze head on. He wasn't the one I hated. He had never noticed me before. He'd not been someone I expected to be better than that. Nash had been. But Ryker Lee had been there. He had said the words. Made the joke. The one that had cut deep enough to change me.

"Well, hello," Ryker Lee said with a drawl. Then as he got closer to me, I saw the confusion in his eyes. Slowly that turned to clarity. He recognized me. "Holy shit," he muttered.

I let him take in my transformation. As he let out a low whistle that I found insulting, Asa said "What is it?" He was still confused.

"Tallulah, right?" Ryker said when his eyes stopped gawking at my body and found my face.

"Yes," I replied.

"Wow" was all he said.

"Tallulah." Asa said my name as if it were familiar, but he just couldn't place it.

"The summer was good to you," Ryker finally said, a slow smile spreading across his face.

I wanted to say that I had in fact worn a bathing suit. But I held that close. He didn't need to know I'd heard him. I also didn't want to hear his apologies.

"Likewise," I said, although I gave him a forced smile. "Have a good day," I added, then walked away. That was done. My first conversation with those close to Nash. As much as I didn't want to talk to them. Ryker had never spoken to me before. Why should I speak to him now? But I had to. My plan was to be accepted into Nash's world and then completely ignore him. Embarrass him in front of his friends. Let him see how it felt. Then, when I was satisfied, I'd walk away from all of that crowd. Find a path that fit me and be happy. But not yet.

"Wait!" Asa called out.

I stopped walking and glanced back at him. "Yes?"

"You're a senior, right?"

It was all I could do not to roll my eyes. I simply nodded.

"What's your first class?"

Seriously? It was this easy? He didn't know me. Had no idea if I was intelligent, had a sense of humor, had any ambition in life. But he saw how I looked in this short skirt, and that was all it took. I had his complete attention.

"Trig," I told him.

His eyebrows shot up. "Gorgeous and smart. We've got that one together. I'll walk with you."

We had been in advanced classes together since ninth grade. Something he didn't recall. But I did.

"Okay," I agreed, then saw Ryker watching me. I gave him a smile and little wave that I assumed was flirty before walking toward the entrance with Asa.

"I'm having a hard time believing we've been in school

together since elementary and I don't remember you. Although your name is familiar."

For a smart boy, you'd think he would realize how admitting he didn't remember me made him seem like a jerk.

"I doubt you notice fat girls." The distaste in my tone was unavoidable. I could only take so much.

"Fat?" he repeated. "You're not fat."

I turned my head until my eyes met his. "No, Asa, not now. Not anymore. But the Tallulah you don't remember was fat."

Slowly I could see the recognition in his eyes. They grew wider, and then his mouth dropped open slightly. Maybe he did remember the fat girl in the corner. My face was thin now, but it had all the same features. If he'd ever taken the time to look at me then, he'd see that.

"You gave me your notes last year when I missed class for a week with the flu," he whispered. Like he was too amazed to talk in his normal tone.

"Yes."

He stared at me then. I wondered how many other memories of me he was recalling. I let him stare. Remember the girl I once was, because that girl was nicer. Kinder. This one wasn't.

This Tallulah was going to leave her mark, then walk away.

CHAPTER 2

NASH

I was late, and I didn't want to be here. Standing outside, staring at this place, all I felt was disappointment, pain, and loss. This was supposed to be my defining year. I had plans. I was a senior. I'd leave here and go become great. Football was my life. It was my future. It was all I'd cared about fighting for since I was old enough to walk around holding a ball in my hands and not falling down.

And all those dreams were gone. Just like that. Over. I hadn't wanted to come back. My dad was making me. Told me life threw shit at you, and how you handled it defined the man you would become. All I knew was my life was over. I didn't want to fucking handle it. I wanted to stay away from here. From what was formerly my life. All my dreams were dead.

The late bell sounded, and I still stood there looking. My friends had been supportive. But the pity in their eyes was almost too much. I hated seeing it there. When I began walking toward the entrance, the limp I'd now live with the rest of my life mocked me. Reminding me of what I'd lost. What could never be again.

The darkness in my soul was taking over. Just two months ago I had been so excited about what would come next. My life was just like I had always planned it. Senior year was ahead and with it my chances at a scholarship at a division one school. Ryker and I had been going to go together. We were a team. We'd play on Saturdays for our family and friends to watch on television. College would be our kingdom.

Ryker would still have that, but my shot was done. I didn't even know what the fuck to do with my life now. Why even go to school? I'd never wanted to do anything in life but play football.

"You going in there, or you going to stand out here and glare at it?"

I turned to see Coach D standing beside me. His hands in his pockets, staring at the school much the same way I had been. He was new. He'd been hired at the end of last year. I hardly knew him. All I knew about him was he was twenty-seven, had played football for Tennessee, and had a teaching degree. He was the defense coordinator on the team.

"Not your business." My tone was angrier than it needed to be. The man had done nothing to me. But he reminded me of all I didn't have now.

"Technically it is. I'm a teacher. One of yours to be exact. I get to correct students. Comes with the gig. Or so they tell me."

He was trying to lighten my mood. I got that a lot these days from people, and I hated it. I hated everything. "I'm already late."

He nodded. "Yeah, you are. So am I. Bad car battery this morning. But then I have a shit car."

We weren't friends. We never even played a game together. By the time practice started up, my leg was already fucked. I didn't want to be his friend, nor did I need someone to talk to. That was coming next. I could feel it in the air. Thick and annoying. He'd offer to listen to me. Tell me he understood. All that bullshit.

I didn't say anything more to him. When he sighed, I felt my teeth grind in anticipation of the next words. His offer to listen. His small pep talk that he could shove up his ass.

"It's my job, so I better go on in. You'll have to give the

place death stares on your own. Good luck with that." That was all he said. Then he walked on. Toward the entrance. Past me. No words of encouragement. Nothing.

"That's it?" I asked before I could stop myself.

He paused and glanced back at me. "What?" He looked confused.

I waved my hand in the direction of the school in frustration I didn't expect to feel. "You're a fucking teacher. I'm out here, and that's all you're gonna say?"

He shrugged. "Sure. You want to stay out here in your own little hell, then do it. Nothing I can say to give you back your old life, Nash. Why waste my breath?"

When he walked off this time, I just stood there watching him. Some would think he was a dick. But for the first time since I . . . I hadn't been talked to like an invalid who needed special care.

Once he was inside, I followed him. No point in protesting. My dad would be up here ready to kick my ass if they called and said I wasn't here. He was as broken up about this as I was. He had dreams. We shared them. But he wasn't gonna let me miss school.

The door was heavier than I remembered. But then all the times I had walked through it before I'd been happy about things. I had liked it here. Now it was taunting me. The Lions crest on the wall with the championship banner from last year flashed like a neon sign. I'd played on that team. Been a part of that victory.

My chest felt like it was being clawed at by sharp talons. The lion mocking me as it loomed ahead. Once I had gotten excited about that crest. I had been a lion.

"You've missed the late bell, Nash," Mrs. Murphy, one of the school secretaries said from the office. The door was always propped open with a large box fan blowing. I turned to look at her. Did she honestly think I didn't know I was late? I'd ruined my damn leg, not my head. It worked just fine.

"Here," she said, walking out of the office and toward me. The sad look in her eyes was something I was familiar with now. She knew, and with her knowledge was the pity. "Take this with you and go on to class."

The piece of paper in her hands was an excuse. I took it. "Thanks," I said, simply because she was old. She'd had white hair back when my parents were in school. I was an asshole these days, but I did draw the line at being mean to the elderly.

She patted my arm. "We all love you here."

That was where I nodded and walked off. I couldn't take the "we love you, we support you, we're rooting for you" speech. Not this morning.

The halls were empty, and I walked slowly. Not because

of the pain from each step but because I dreaded facing them. They'd all know. They'd all look at me differently. The guy I had been was no longer, and that made for something to gawk at. To whisper about.

Blakely and I had been an item. Just after school ended, we had hooked up at a field party. I liked her. Or I had. She was fun, exciting, and she had no problem crawling in the back of my Escalade with me. I thought we had something. But like everything else, my injury changed it all. She came around a lot at first, then after a couple weeks of therapy she slowly began to fade away.

I hadn't heard from her in two weeks. I had texted her and got nothing. I saw from her Snapchats that she was living life. She just didn't have time to reply to me. I accepted it as part of what would become my life now.

Just When I Thought
I'd Get My Revenge

CHAPTER 3

TALLULAH

Three classes and still no sign of Nash. I hated that it was what had driven me to lose weight. That my hurt and disappointment in him had made me walk every day. Because I wanted to be proud of what I'd done. I was healthier. I had more energy. I felt confident. But I hadn't achieved all this for me.

"You decided on a college yet?" Asa asked. Once again he was there beside me. He'd barely left my side all day. It was annoying.

"Not yet," I replied. I had it down to three different colleges. My ACT score last year had been a 29, and that was high enough for all the colleges I was interested in.

However, I was going to take it one more time to see if I could get it up to a 30.

"I want to go to Ole Miss. Hoping I can get the attention of their scouts this season," Asa said, looking more confident than he should. The only guy on the team I expected to get a football scholarship was Nash. The others were good, but the stars had graduated this past May.

"They've got a beautiful campus" was all I could think to say. Mississippi was too close to Alabama. Not far enough away from here for me. I was going northeast or west. I hadn't yet made that decision. But it would be far away.

He chuckled as if my comment was amusing. "I guess. But what really matters is their football program."

"Most guys here dream of Alabama." I stated the obvious.

He shrugged. "I'll never be a star there. I'd never get a chance. Too much competition."

I had to agree with him, but Ole Miss wasn't exactly easy either. Wasn't my business, so I just kept my mouth shut.

"Nash! Where you been?" Asa called out, and instantly my heart picked up its pace. I didn't want to look his way. He didn't need to see me looking for him. Just because my heart still went a little silly over his name didn't mean my head did.

When Nash didn't respond, Asa sighed heavily. "I need to go talk to him."

I had to bite my tongue to keep from asking why. Nash was always happy and friendly. I gave in slightly and peeked in the direction of Asa's gaze. Nash's eyes were cold—or were they empty?—as he looked straight ahead. He wasn't the smiling guy I remembered. Actually, I had never seen him so . . . angry.

"I'll find you later. Lunch?" he asked, moving in Nash's direction.

I almost replied that I'd be in the library, reading. That's where I wanted to be. But this year I was going to be different. I nodded. "Sure."

He shot me a giant grin, then headed toward Nash. The crowd in the hallway had almost blocked him from view. Asa fought through the bodies, and I looked away. I wouldn't let Nash see me looking at him. I'd ignore him. That was the plan. To make him feel unimportant. Invisible. To make him feel like I had felt.

"Tallulah," a female voice said, and I turned my attention to the left of me. Mary Dees, the senior class president and one of the only girls in our class who seemed to know me, was smiling at me.

"Hello," I replied.

She beamed brightly. Mary was always happy. She was

in charge of every charity event the school held and editor of the yearbook, and I was pretty sure she read to the preschoolers at the library twice a week.

"You look amazing. It took me a moment to figure out who you were." She sincerely meant this as a compliment. In ninth grade she wrote a paper about how on Thanksgiving she and her family went to the homeless shelter and served dinner to the people there. She explained how rewarding it was and encouraged others to do the same. There wasn't a mean bone in the girl's body.

"Thank you," I replied.

"I didn't mean you weren't beautiful before. You were. You've always had amazing hair, and those eyes of yours are stunning. I just meant, you really stand out now." She paused and frowned. "I think that made it worse. I am not saying this right."

"It's okay. I know what you mean," I assured her.

She looked relieved. "Good. I debated saying anything at all for fear it would come out wrong. It's just everyone is going on and on about the 'new girl,' and it annoys me. You're not new. We go to school with a lot of blind people."

"Yes we do," I agreed.

"I'll see you later. This is my stop," she said, then gave me a little wave before turning in to the senior Lit class.

I was almost to my class when I felt someone's gaze on

was no one, she was done

a said as he came up beside
I knew his voice.
ed. With fucking daily strength-
bilitation. Not that he or anyone

ed."
of acknowledgment. He didn't get it.
y still had their plans. Their futures. I

is is Nash Lee. He's normally friendlier,"
I turned my head then to look at the girl he
ing. I knew Tallulah. She was kind, quiet, and

rl I saw beside him wasn't the girl I remembered.
the girl I'd noticed in the hall earlier. The strikingly
ul blonde. I stopped walking for a moment and
tared. Was that the same Tallulah? I studied her eyes
realized it was. She'd lost weight. The face I'd always
ought was pretty was now beautiful.

"You look good," I said to her, ignoring Asa. We'd been
in school with Tallulah since we were kids. He didn't need
to introduce her to me as if her new body made her a new
person.

me. I turned my head, and my eyes locked with Nash's. There was no gleam. No sparkle of fun. Instead there was pain. Sorrow. Anger. Confused, I wasn't able to look away. But he did. He turned around and went into a room. No smile. Nothing.

I stood there watching his back until it disappeared into the room. Then I stood there a moment longer. What was wrong with Nash Lee? This was not how I had imagined this moment. And I had played this scenario over in my head a million times while walking in the summer heat. It drove me daily, as did his laughter at a cruel remark said about me. But that Nash . . . he wasn't the Nash I had expected. No flirty smile. Nothing.

I wasn't friends with these people on social media. I kept to myself. No one told me things. But something was definitely different. Others didn't seem to think it was odd. Asa had seemed to accept it easily enough. So what was I missing?

The warning bell sounded, and I tore my gaze from the now closed door that Nash had entered. Quickly I made it to my next class before the late bell. But my mind was on Nash Lee. It seemed to always be on Nash. Just when I thought I'd get my revenge and move on, something happened and it all changed.

Other than Nash staring at me for a moment, I had

been all but invisible to him. Or unimportant. He'd always spoken to me in the past. Always been kind. Now that I looked like the girls he dated, he had nothing to say to me.

"You got this class next?" Ryker asked with a flirty grin. One I was used to seeing on his cousin.

"Yes," I replied.

"Good. It just got a hell of a lot better." That was a stupid comment. One I was sure that worked on girls all the time. But not me. I was the fat girl he hoped didn't wear a bathing suit. I wouldn't forget that, even though he obviously had.

We've Been in th
Grade since Eleme

CHAPTE

NASH

Blakely wasn't in any of my clas
I saw her. She was flirting with H
able. He was the quarterback now tha
graduated. He was also a junior. Blakely

Hunter saw me just as Blakely leaned
ing off her cleavage. It was one of her mo
tures. I saw him immediately tense and witho
interaction he'd obviously been enjoying.

There was no way I was letting him or he
cared. But I did. It stung. This was just one more r
of how different my life was. Blakely and I hadn't be
damn special after all. It had been who I was that attrac

She studied me a moment as if she wasn't sure what to say or do with this Nash. The one who limped when he walked and scowled at the world. I held her gaze and then began walking again. It was Asa who said something next.

"You know each other?" was his brilliant response.

I didn't look at either of them. I kept my gaze focused on the cafeteria door. "Of course we do. We've been in the same damn grade since elementary school," I replied with disgust.

"Yeah, but—" Asa started to say something stupid and caught himself.

I didn't want to do this with them. I didn't want to fucking be here. Good for Tallulah. She'd lost weight. Got herself a new life. Was attracting the attention of a winner like Asa. I hope it was all she'd dreamed of.

"Are you hurt?" Tallulah asked. If it had been anyone else, I'd have snapped. Because the whole fucking town had heard of my injury by now. Except possibly Tallulah. I paused, turned my head slightly, and saw the sincere concern—or was it confusion?—in her expression. She may be the one person who didn't know about my accident.

"Not a good topic," Asa said quickly.

"No," I said instead. "I'm fucking ruined." Then I left them there. Knowing they could see my limp. That people were watching me, pitying me, thankful they weren't me.

She'd been asking an innocent question. I knew Asa would give her the details. Just as I knew Asa would work her until he was satisfied he'd had enough. She was too naïve to be careful with a guy like him. If I had a heart, I'd warn her. Try and help her out. I just didn't have enough left in me to give a shit. Besides, lessons learned the hard way were good for you. At least that's what my dad said.

"Nash!" Tallulah called out. I wanted to ignore her. Keep going. Get this living hell also known as lunch over with. But hearing her voice, I saw the shy, overweight girl who was afraid to be seen. Afraid to speak up. She wasn't that girl anymore. She had a confidence now that she deserved. Still . . . I stopped and turned around.

"Yeah," I replied, wishing I'd just ignored her.

She didn't say anything. She just looked at me. As if she needed to study me, figure this out. I wasn't a damn sideshow. I started to walk off when she took a step toward me. Her eyes had always been big and a dark royal blue behind the glasses she once wore. Now that she was wearing contacts, they were hard to ignore. There wasn't curiosity, pain, or what I hated the most—pity—in her dark blue depths. But there was something I didn't understand. And it wasn't pleasant.

"Words matter," she blurted out. As if that made sense. My words mattered? Well so did my fucking leg. It mattered. It mattered a hell of a lot more than my words.

Since I had no pleasant response to that, I turned and walked into the cafeteria. Blakely was there at our table. Or the football team's table. Was it even mine anymore? Didn't matter. She was there. Smiling in my direction. I didn't return her smile. I had no smile to give.

My appetite was gone, but it was that way most of the time now. I'd lost seven pounds since my injury. Eating had become a chore. One I dreaded.

"She called?" Ryker asked.

I turned my head to look at my cousin, who was now beside me. "No."

He shot her a disgusted look. "Never liked her."

That was a lie. He'd liked her just fine at the beginning of the summer. He'd said I had hit the fucking jackpot. We had laughed about it. Thought it was luck. Even said she'd be a hot mom one day and definite marriage material. We'd been so damn shallow.

"I'm a cripple. Can't expect her to stay with me." Even as I said it, I didn't want to think it. Admitting the truth was hard. It hurt like hell. But since I'd been told I would never play football again, I had learned to accept reality. And move on.

"Jesus, Nash, don't call yourself that. You're not a cripple." Ryker was upset. Didn't matter. He needed to face the truth. It was time for us all to grow up.

"I'll never walk normal again."

He frowned. "But you can walk. You can walk, Nash. You can fucking walk. That's what you keep forgetting. That's what you need to remember."

I knew he meant well. My parents had said the same thing, minus the cursing. But it pissed me off. It was easy for those who didn't face my reality to say. They had lost nothing. Spouting positive shit was easy for them.

"Don't remind me what I have when you've lost nothing," I said, then turned and walked right back out of the cafeteria. I wasn't hungry anyway. Facing Blakely and her bullshit, my friends and their acting like life was the same was all something I couldn't handle today. Maybe tomorrow. But not today.

I Had Always Been Trying
to Climb That Dang Rope
and Never Getting Anywhere

CHAPTER 5

TALLULAH

I watched them. I tried not to, but it was hard to ignore. Nash was different, and Ryker seemed angry about it. When Nash stalked out of the cafeteria, I noticed it then. He was limping. I'd noticed something was wrong earlier, but I hadn't realized it was so severe. I watched him until he was gone. Until the door swung closed behind him. Then I quickly turned my gaze away before Ryker caught me staring.

Asa was busy getting his burger buried in toppings. He hadn't noticed any of it. I wanted to ask. I was missing something. Two things were obvious. Nash was angry, and he was hurt. That much I had figured out.

"You gonna eat?" Asa asked, finally glancing up from the burger he'd made into a mountain.

"Yes, but we aren't at the salad bar yet," I replied. He'd held up the line working on his burger.

He smirked. "Takes me a while to get this baby right. A burger is a masterpiece. A fucking work of art."

I glanced back to see Ryker still standing where Nash had left him. He was glaring toward the door as if he wasn't sure what he was going to do next. Go after him or just let him go.

"Nash isn't handling it well," Asa said. "Ryker's worried about him."

I turned back to Asa. I'd been caught staring. Might as well not try and cover it up now. "What isn't he handling well?" I asked.

Asa frowned. "His injury. He won't play football again. Changed his life in one bad tackle." He shook his head. "It's not fair. I hate it for him."

The limp was more than a sprained ankle apparently. "It won't heal?" I asked, thinking they sounded a bit more dramatic than it appeared. Nash was just limping. He'd get over that eventually.

"He's as healed as it's going to get."

I started to ask exactly what had happened when Ryker stepped between us. "I can't talk to him. You go," he said to Asa. "I want to fucking knock some sense into him. He's getting worse rather than better and that—" Ryker shot a disgusted look over at Blakely. "She isn't helping. Heartless bitch."

I had never seen Ryker Lee angry. Much like Nash, he was always joking, smiling, and enjoying his life. This was all very different. The summer hadn't just changed me. It had changed the Lee cousins too.

"He needs time." Asa sounded like he knew what he was talking about.

Ryker sighed. "I wish Brady was here. He listened to Brady." Brady Higgens had been the quarterback all-around good guy who was loved by one and all. But he'd graduated in the spring. I wasn't sure what college he'd gone off to. I didn't keep up with that kind of thing. Or anything for that matter. Since I didn't even know Nash had been hurt, that was kind of obvious. My world outside of school was a small bubble. Me, my mom, my books, my house. Not much else. Although I knew my mother hoped that would all change for me this year. She was a social butterfly. My hermit life bothered her.

But then my mother was five foot five, 118 pounds, with a bubbly personality and a head full of blond curls. She was wildly creative and upbeat. Our oddly painted house was testimony to her personality. People loved her.

She was hard not to love. I wasn't my mother. Many times in life I had wished I was.

"Just give him space. Today is hard. It's like he had to face it all over again. He needs time to adjust."

Ryker finally sighed. His shoulders drooped, and he looked defeated. The obvious love and concern he had for his cousin was touching. For a moment I almost forgot that it was his cruel words that had caused this . . . this new me. That I had suffered cruelty from the one guy I never expected it from and that was all because of Ryker. Standing there, I reminded myself not to feel pity. Not to feel sympathy. Not to feel. Because he hadn't felt that for me. He didn't even know who I was or remember what he had said.

I was that unimportant.

My defenses were back up. My moment of weakness ended. I had a purpose. I would enjoy this year. I'd live it like I wouldn't get another, because the truth was I wouldn't. This was the last year of high school. I had me to worry about. Not an injured Nash Lee. So his girlfriend broke his heart. Well boohoo. He'd broken mine. I was sure he'd also broken dozens of hearts. Now he was just getting a dose of it himself. And poor little Ryker Lee. His world wasn't perfect. He couldn't enjoy himself because his cousin was sad. Guess he'll figure out life ain't roses after all.

I plastered a smile on my face. "Excuse me, I need to get my salad," I said, and stepped around both of them. Walking away, I felt empowered. I wasn't letting my softness win. I was tossing their troubles aside and going to enjoy my day. My year.

Okay, so I felt like a bitch. But again, whose fault was that? Ugly words. Cruel words. Laughter at my expense. They hadn't lost any sleep over it. They forgot it even happened moments after it was said. While I was walking in the heat of the day and drinking a gallon of water daily and counting my calories, those words and that laughter haunted me.

No. I wouldn't feel sorry for Nash and his injury. So he didn't get his college football career. Well, it could be worse. He had a brain still. He could do something else. And Ryker acting like he needed to be sheltered from the pain of disappointment. They both needed a dose of reality. Neither had experienced it until now.

They should try going to PE and knowing it was the day everyone had to climb the rope. The PE teacher was going to stand there and watch everyone. Use a stopwatch to see how fast we could climb the rope. See who could get to the top. And know that I couldn't move an inch up that rope. Everyone would see me hanging there, wishing I could climb even a little. The snickers from the others would make my cheeks red. I would start to sweat, and my stomach would feel sick. I'd wish to be anywhere but there. The PE teacher would tell me to try harder. I could do it. But I couldn't. My arms would never be strong enough to pull my weight up that rope. So . . . I'd give up. Humiliated. Unable to look anyone in the eye. Giggles and whispers would grow louder. The teacher would tell the others to stop. But it didn't go away. I never forgot. That was my life. I had always been trying to climb that dang rope and never getting anywhere.

Not once did Nash or Ryker worry about me.

I fixed my salad. I got a cup of water. And I went outside. To a table to be alone. Because right now I wasn't exactly happy with myself. Although I knew I was right. I just didn't like the way right made me feel.

CHAPTER 6

NASH

I tossed my book bag onto my bed and glared at it like it had done something wrong. I was home on the first day of school at three fifteen in the afternoon. This was a first. I should be at the field house. Changing into my pads. Making bad jokes with my friends. Practicing in the heat until I vomited. That was what I was supposed to be doing.

But I was here.

In my living nightmare. With absolutely nothing to do. There was homework. Reading that was mandatory. Physical therapy in an hour. Bullshit, bullshit, and more bullshit.

"Hey, baby." My mother's voice startled me. She was normally at work until five. I turned to see her standing at my door. Concern, pain, and a trace of hope in her eyes. She wanted me to be better. To find happiness with the way my life was now.

"Why are you home?" I asked, already knowing the answer. My mother who never took off from work or left early was here because of me.

"Oh, I took off early. Thought I could make you a chocolate cream pie before you go to therapy. Maybe talk about your day." Her voice was cautious. She didn't want to upset me. I'd been a pill to live with this summer. Since the accident at least.

"Not hungry. My day sucked." She had wanted to hear something else. Something positive. I didn't have anything positive to tell her, though. Not one damn thing. This was our reality. She needed to deal with it.

"It'll get better," she said softly. She wanted it to get better. She hoped it would. My mother was an eternal optimist. I had been one too, once. But not anymore.

"No. It won't. I'm not going to run again. I'm going to walk with this limp. I'll never play ball again. So no, Mom, it's not going to get better. There is no light in my future."

Her shoulders dropped, her face sad. I hated that it was me making her feel this way. But I just didn't have the energy to make her smile. She liked to be happy. I did too. But that wasn't happening again. It was all gone.

"You sure you don't want some pie?"

One thing about mom was you couldn't completely knock her off course. She held on until the bitter end. As for me, she hadn't let go yet.

"Therapy is hard. It hurts, and if I eat pie before I go, I'll vomit during therapy." More reality. More truth. More of what she liked to pretend wasn't happening.

"Okay. Well I'll make some for later. It can be a treat for after. I'll be in the kitchen if you want to talk. I'm always here to listen."

"Thanks," I managed to say. Simply because I hated hurting her. She started to leave but then stopped, came into the room, and hugged me tightly.

"I love you. I won't let you give up. I'm your momma. I will never ever give up on you. You've got a big future, Nash Lee. A huge one. This is just a stumbling block. It'll make you tough, stronger, and more determined."

I just nodded and hugged her back. She needed to believe it, and I let her. No reason to make her as miserable as me. When she finally let me go, she patted my cheek, as if I were five inches shorter than her rather than the five inches I towered over her.

"Do your homework. Focus on your grades. You'll do great things," she said, then left the room, finally leaving me to my peace.

If I could think like my mother, maybe I wouldn't be so damn miserable. Today had been a slap in the face. From seeing the guys I'd played ball with laughing and cutting up like we always had, to seeing excitement in the halls for Friday night's game, to seeing Blakely hugged up on Hunter—all of it reminded me I wasn't Nash Lee anymore. I was just another face in the crowd. Someone others would rather whisper about, force a smile at, and move on along.

That was what my day was like. That was what my mother needed to hear, but I couldn't say that to her. She'd worry about it. Worry about me. She'd not get any sleep. I would have her hovering more than she already was. Keeping all that inside was how I had to deal with it.

I was standing at the window going over all this shit in my head when my dad's truck pulled up outside. He should be at work until seven. But here he was, just like my mother, coming home early. To ask me questions I wasn't going to answer. To give me another pep talk. I wasn't in the mood for this. Grabbing my car keys off the bed, I headed for the back door. Away from the kitchen. Away from the way my dad would enter the house. Once I was safely outside and I knew he'd entered the house, I hurried to my Escalade and left.

Dad would call me once he realized I'd left without saying anything. He'd bitch. I'd listen. Then it would be over.

I still had forty-five minutes before I had to be at physical therapy. I had nowhere to go. Nothing to do. Dad had suggested I get a job. It was more than a suggestion. It was a demand. I could go put in some applications. That would at least give me somewhere to be other than the house every afternoon.

Driving toward town, I saw her. Walking down the side of the street. I'd seen her today. She'd been impossible to miss. Tallulah Liddell had transformed over the summer. Even when we'd been kids, she'd struggled with her weight. Her sweet smile and kind heart, however, had shown brightly. It made her hard to overlook. Seeing her now, though, I could tell there was something missing.

Pulling over, I rolled down my window. "Need a ride?" I asked, surprising myself.

She paused and glanced at me. "No. I walk five miles every day. This is on purpose."

Oh. Well that explained the weight loss. "Impressive," I replied.

She frowned. Studied me a moment, then shook her head as if she was baffled by me. "Is it? The fat girl started exercising. That's impressive to you?" Definite disgust in her tone.

What the hell had I done to her? Far as I could recall, I'd been the only guy, or girl for that matter, who was nice to her. I didn't ignore her. I had spoken to her often. She'd been so timid and shy, like she was hiding from the world. But I wouldn't let her. I made sure she knew I saw her.

"Got a chip on your thin shoulders?" I asked, annoyed. I wasn't in the mood for this. Why had I even stopped?

She jerked her head back in my direction. Anger flashing in her startling, attractive blue eyes. "Yes. I do. But then that's why I walk. Why I started." With that response she walked on, leaving me behind. Parked there on the side of the street like I'd done something to her. Jesus, what was her deal? She was thin, beautiful, and every guy at school had been drooling over her today. Wasn't that all she wanted? Why she'd walked herself thin? At least she wasn't fucking limping around getting sympathy looks.

I started to drive off and changed my mind. I turned off the engine and got out. I needed a confrontation. I had enough anger in me to take on Tallulah Liddell and her issues. With the slamming of my car door, she stopped and looked back at me.

I had her attention now.

"What the fuck is wrong with you? Did losing weight turn you into a bitch? If that's your problem, then go eat a box of cookies. You were a helluva lot nicer when you ate. Being thin and wearing short skirts doesn't give you the right to be rude." As I yelled at her, I wondered why I was

LOSING THE FIELD   43

doing this. What was the point? I didn't care how Tallulah acted. I had bigger problems in my life.

She took a step toward me. Her eyes were flashing with fury now. Well past anger. "No, Nash Lee, losing weight didn't turn me into a bitch. You did."

CHAPTER 7

TALLULAH

That might have been an unfair statement. Technically, he hadn't turned me into a bitch. His actions had an impact on my anger, drive for revenge, and current state of mind. My health was better. My doctor had said as much. No longer was I at risk for type 2 diabetes. If I was honest with myself, that should have been reason enough for me to exercise and choose healthier foods. Instead, it had taken being made fun of by the one guy I liked.

Nash shook his head and let out a hard laugh. "Really? I'd love to hear how I am to blame for your current personality faults." He was looking at me like I was insane. I was starting to feel that way.

My reasons seemed ridiculous now. Telling him that he had laughed at a fat joke about me seemed silly. Embarrassing. It also let him know how much his actions affected me. No one needed that kind of power.

"Nothing. Forget I said anything," I snapped, then started walking again. Hoping he'd get in his stupid silver Escalade, that I had once dreamed of riding in, and drive away. Let this go.

"I'm to blame for a lot of shit, Tallulah. But being unkind to you was never one of those things. I've been nothing but nice to you." Up until that moment last May, I would have agreed with him.

I kept walking. I didn't look back. Doing so meant I had to explain myself. My anger toward him. I would not do that. He didn't deserve it. After a few moments, and hearing nothing else from him, I chanced a glance in his direction. He was walking—no, he was limping—back to his car. I watched as his once confident swagger was now one that looked painful. Complicated.

Even after all that had happened since the last day of school, my chest still ached watching him. Seeing him struggle like that wasn't easy. I felt guilty for being so mean. For holding that one thing against him. He was hurting, he was angry, and, oddly, he seemed alone. I knew he had friends who worried about him. I witnessed

Ryker and Asa today reaching out to him. But still . . . he seemed alone.

His friends hadn't lost their ability to play football. Their lives hadn't changed. It was Nash facing that. I had been lonely most of my life. I was fine with it, but I knew Nash Lee had never been alone. He'd been king of the world. Full of life and always at the party. This was more than an adjustment for him. It was a nightmare he wouldn't wake up from.

When he got in his Escalade, I looked away before he saw me. I walked on. Trying not to care what I saw. Not to worry about Nash or feel bad for him. That seemed impossible, though.

By the time I reached my driveway, it was after six, and I'd walked over seven miles today. Every time I thought I was done, I walked some more. Needing to think about things. Decide if this revenge thing was worth it. Or pointless.

The fancy black truck that I knew belonged to Asa was parked outside my house, and Asa was leaning up against it with his arms crossed over his chest and a grin on his face when I spotted him. Football practice was over. And he was here. Looking for me.

This was what I wanted. Or this was what I had wanted. Once. But I'd thought about it all while walking for almost three hours, and I wasn't sure what I wanted now. Because a good book and being alone sounded rather nice to me.

"How far did you walk?" was his first question when I was close enough to hear him.

"Seven miles. Maybe a little more."

His eyebrows shot up. "Damn. I don't think I've walked that much at one time in my life."

I shrugged. There had been many days in the heat of the summer I'd walked ten miles. I enjoyed the solitude of walking. Me and my thoughts alone again. And I wondered if Nash would ever find joy in that, or if he'd always need people around him.

"You do that every day?"

I shook my head. "No. Some days I walk ten; some days I walk five. It's always different."

He nodded as if that made sense, but I doubt he understood it at all.

"I came by to see if you'd like to go over to Ryker's with me. Guys decided to get Nash and force him to hang out tonight. Small party that will probably be moved to the field if too many people show up. But it's a party, so who cares," he finished with a smile that clearly stated he thought he was funny.

I didn't think Nash wanted a party. Had they not all noticed he was suffering today? Did he look like a guy who wanted to be around a bunch of people who didn't understand what he was going through? No. I would be surprised if Ryker could even get Nash to his house. Unless they picked him up and carried him. Force would be the only way.

"Nash didn't seem to be in the mood for a party today," I pointed out.

Asa shrugged. "Yeah. I know. But Ryker is like Nash's brother. They're closer than cousins. Always have been. If anyone can get Nash to socialize, it's Ryker."

I wasn't convinced of this. But the fat girl inside me who knew what it was like to be alone, who knew what it was like to feel as if you don't fit in. As if no one understands you. That girl nodded her head. "Okay. Can I get a quick shower?"

Asa beamed as if I was doing this to be with him. I guess in his eyes this was a date. I hadn't thought of it that way. I'd never been on a date. I didn't want to start tonight. I was going because, whether he realized it or not, Nash Lee was going to need me. I was the only person who understood him, who saw past what they believed he was feeling and got to the core. Maybe he didn't deserve my help because of his laughing at the idea of me in a swimsuit. But then maybe he did. He was nice to me for years when no one else was. I couldn't forget that.

"Sure. I can wait," he replied.

"My mom is going to want to feed you. If you like baked goods, then you're in luck. She's been on Pinterest this past month trying out every bread, pie, cake, and cookie she can find. We never eat them, so she takes them to work. But she'll love having someone she can feed."

Asa seemed excited about that. "I'm starved."

"Then you'll love each other," I told him.

I led him to the front door, then opened it, and sure enough the smell of something fattening and sweet met my nose. "She's already at it. I think this is how she handles work stress."

Asa chuckled. "Seems like a good way to handle stress. Wish this was what my momma did. Instead she watches a lot of sappy shit on television and drinks too much wine."

"Talli! You're home! Come tell me all about your day. I've been waiting for hours. What did you do, walk a marathon? You should have known I would be here anxious to hear all about it. I've made enough cinnamon sugar muffins to feed the entire building tomorrow. Not just my office." My mother stopped talking when she stepped around the corner with her pink apron on, and the smile on her face froze, then grew instantly as she spotted Asa behind me.

"Momma this is Asa Griffith. I'm going to get a shower and go with him to a party at Ryker Lee's house. In the meantime can you feed him? He's starving."

Mom's eyes went wide. She had expected my day to be much different from the past. But I was sure she hadn't been prepared for this. "Of course, I've got several things to choose from. Or you can taste it all," she told him.

I glanced back at him and smiled. "I'll be quick."

He shrugged. "No hurry. That kitchen smells like heaven. Whoa . . . are those clouds painted on your ceiling?"

"Yes they are. Come see the kitchen ceiling. It's even better. My favorite," mom replied with pride.

They would get along just fine. Mom could feed him and show him her painted ceilings.

It Almost Made Her Sudden
Hate for Me Make Sense—Almost

CHAPTER 8

NASH

Ryker wouldn't let it go. He kept pushing until I gave in and went out with him. I knew going meant we wouldn't be alone. When we passed his house and headed back to the field, I sighed. It was a fucking party. I didn't want to go to a damn field party. Another reminder of the life I no longer had.

"You know this is the last thing I want to do," I told him.

"Yeah. But you sitting your ass at home sulking isn't healthy. This is."

I shook my head and glared out the window of his truck. "Just let me deal with this my way. Stop trying to help me face it. You don't know what this is like."

Ryker didn't respond right away. "Maybe not," he finally said. "I just hate to see you sit here."

"I need time."

"You've had plenty of time. You've had a fucking summer's worth of time."

If I didn't love him, I'd throw his ass out of this moving vehicle. When we got to the field, I would just walk the eight miles home. Better than putting up with this. Besides, it was a Monday night. Not a field party night. We didn't party on Monday nights during the school year. This was all about me. Them trying to make me act like the Nash I had been. Didn't they get it? He was gone.

Cars, trucks, and a few Jeeps all filled the parking space among the trees. I recognized most all of them. The ones I didn't had to be new vehicles. Those who had gotten their licenses over the summer. I laid my head back on the seat and groaned. "I don't want to do this."

"You need this. To remember it's not over. We are all still here. We all miss you. Football doesn't define you."

Angry, my head snapped up and I glared at him. "Does it define you? It's all we've ever known. But it wasn't taken from you. If it was gone tomorrow, what then?"

Ryker shrugged. "I'd find another path. Move on. I don't love it the way you do, Nash. Never have. It's just football. It's not my life."

That was easy for him to say. He wasn't in my shoes. It wasn't out of his reach. Never would be. I slung the door open and climbed out. Staring down the road, I considered doing what I had planned: walking home.

But the look on my dad's face if I did made me pause. I was sure he knew exactly where I was and supported it. I didn't want to face him any more than I did this damn party.

"Did you invite the whole fucking school?" I snarled.

"Yeah. Now stop being a dick and come drink a beer. Relax. Enjoy yourself."

They were drinking beer on a Monday night before their first game of the season Friday. They needed to practice all week. Stay focused. Get rest. Not drink beer for God's sake. Did they all think so little of what they had? What they could have? Had I taken it for granted like this?

"It's one beer. Stop acting like Coach," Ryker replied, reading my thoughts.

Without much other choice I walked beside him through the trees with only the moonlight guiding our path. We didn't need any light. These woods had been our childhood. We knew them well.

As we stepped through the tree line and into the open field where a fire pit was already going, cheers arose. They were acting like I'd won some damn award. I heard my name called out a few times. I didn't even try to respond.

That beer was sounding better. After all, I wouldn't be playing football on Friday. I didn't need to prepare.

"They are here for you," Ryker said, as if I needed clarification.

"I know that," I snapped.

"Then act like you give a shit."

I was tired of him trying to force this on me. He needed me to act the way I always had so he wouldn't have to face reality. We wouldn't be going to college together. We wouldn't be playing ball together again. Those were the hard truths. I'd faced it, and he needed to now. This hanging on to a fantasy was annoying.

"I don't," I replied. Then I walked on. Away from my cousin, who I knew meant well but was pushing too hard. I needed space.

"Nash!" a voice called out. I turned to see Asa standing over by the bed of his truck with Rifle Hannon, Hunter Maclay, and Walker McNair. All guys I would have started with this year. Guys I would never get that close to. A team I wouldn't be a part of.

I glanced at Hunter one more time to see if Blakely was anywhere near him. I didn't see her. But my eyes locked on one female. One I wasn't in the mood to see as much as I wasn't in the mood for this party. Tallulah. All that blond hair hanging down around her shoulders. Long legs barely covered by the shorts she was wearing, and those eyes. Damn expressive. I hated that I was attracted to her.

It wasn't that I disliked her. I'd always liked Tallulah. I just hated that the fact I was suddenly attracted to her in a way I had never been was because she had lost weight. It almost made her sudden hate for me make sense. Almost.

She wasn't angry with Asa for being all over her. She forgave him for never noticing her in the past. But me, she was furious with me. It annoyed me. Along with everything else in life.

"We need to talk," Blakely said, snapping me out of my thoughts and away from Tallulah. I turned to see her standing to my left. Barely dressed and stunning. Like always.

"Now you want to talk?" I asked. She sure hadn't been interested in it this summer.

She rolled her eyes. "Don't go blaming this on me. You changed. You got so . . . dark and angry. I couldn't deal with that. I don't like to be unhappy."

I stood there and listened to her tell me how my suffering had been bad for her vibe. I shouldn't be shocked. I'd been the one to date her knowing she was particularly selfish. I'd known her for years. She wasn't one to be labeled as kind and caring. More like wild and exciting.

"Then what do we have to talk about?" I asked, deciding that walking home wasn't such a bad idea.

"Us. We aren't working."

I laughed then. Did she think I needed to be told this? Either her intelligence was lacking, or she thought my head had been injured along with my leg. "No kidding."

Her eyes flared, as did her nostrils. "You don't have to be an ass."

"I'm not. Just find it funny you think I thought there was an us. We haven't talked in weeks. Besides . . ." I nodded my head in Hunter's direction. "You've got a junior to break in."

She made a disgusted sound. "You're a jerk. I shouldn't have even tried to talk to you. There is no point."

I agreed. She shouldn't. "Then don't."

That was enough to send her stalking off in a pair of heels not meant for the grass. She managed to walk in them anyway. I could follow her and make everyone in that group uncomfortable. Say shit to make them wince. But I didn't feel like wasting my time.

I moved toward the beer once again when headlights broke through the trees and caught everyone's attention. Confused, I turned to watch as a shitty car pulled into the clearing.

When Coach D stepped out, the entire field went silent. What the hell was he doing here?

Well, Please, by All Means,
Call the Police

CHAPTER 9

TALLULAH

"Shit, why's he here?" Asa muttered, drawing my attention off Nash and toward where everyone else seemed to be looking.

My new English Literature teacher, Mr. Dace. Also known as Coach D. I had that class with a few football players. They had referred to him as such. He didn't look or act like the other football coaches. He was younger, better-looking, and had a bit of a nerdy, cool persona. I enjoyed his class today. It had been an introduction to what was to come mostly, but he seemed to love the idea of teaching.

The last time I had a coach for a teacher had been

Driver's Ed in tenth grade. This was different. Mr. Dace was the first coach who taught something that required a solid degree in our school. I saw him talking to Ryker, who seemed furious that he was here. This was the Lees' land. Their grandfather and fathers knew about the parties. They were allowed. No adult had ever come back here that I knew of. But then again, this was my first party too.

"Why is Coach D here?" Hunter asked, a touch of concern in his tone. It was as if he were about to face a cop with that cup of beer in his underage hand instead of his coach. I wondered if Hunter had ever been in a lot of trouble. It didn't seem like it. But then, I didn't know much about Hunter, or any of the team. To be honest, I knew very little about anyone at our school.

"Shit, there goes Nash," Asa said, standing up from the tailgate he'd been sitting on. "I better go help." He glanced at me. "Let's go."

I didn't exactly want to stay here with these people I didn't know, so I did as told. I went with him. Mr. Dace appeared laid-back as he listened to Ryker talk, but then his eyebrows shot up just as we got close enough to hear them.

"You think this is going to win any games? This

behavior? I understand this is the norm on a Friday night after a game. But starting this on a Monday when we have a week to prepare and get our minds ready?" Mr. Dace waved his hand at the crowd now watching the conversation.

"What I think is that this is the way we handle things. Coaches have never bothered us here before," Ryker said, his tone still respectful but firm.

"He's right," Nash said loudly, holding up a red plastic cup full of beer. It sloshed over the rim. "If y'all want to win, you don't need to be here kissing my ass. Trying to act like my fucking world isn't over. Listen to the man," he told Ryker. Then he turned his eyes toward Mr. Dace. "As for you, get off. This is private property. You weren't invited on it. Now leave. Don't come back."

I halted in my steps. Nash's tone had gone from nice to nasty in a split second. He was glaring at Mr. Dace as if he was the one at fault here. Not the field full of under-age teens drinking beer. I wasn't so sure there weren't some things being smoked, either. I didn't know what that looked or smelled like, so I wasn't positive.

"Might be private property, but if I call the cops, they'll only care about the teens consuming alcohol and the smell of weed in the air."

Ryker muttered something, then turned to stand between

Mr. Dace and Nash with his back to Mr. Dace. "Just let it go. Last thing we need is the police showing up here."

Nash laughed loudly. "You think they'd actually come? Hell, these parties have been going on since our dads were teens. The cops know. They don't fucking care. They just want the football team to win. More important than some teens drinking a beer." He leaned to the side and smiled at Mr. Dace. "Wouldn't you agree? No? Well please, by all means, call the police. Find out how this town works."

"Shut up," Ryker snarled at Nash.

Nash beamed at him. The bright fake smile that meant nothing. "Why? You wanted me to get out and have fun. This is fun. Best time I've had all summer. Seeing him call the cops would be even more entertaining."

Nash's voice was loud now. I knew everyone could hear him. I took a glance around and saw people leaving. Some quickly. Others trying to do so quietly. Hunter Maclay was gone. I guess the quarterback didn't want to get mixed up with this.

"You're scaring them away. Damn, guess we all need to go home now," Nash said, looking anything but disappointed.

"He's had more than his share of beer. Who's sober enough to drive him home?" Mr. Dace asked.

"They've all been drinking," Nash said with a laugh.

"This is my first cup, and I've had one sip. I'm the safest driver here at the moment.

Mr. Dace frowned as if he wasn't so sure about that. But I had seen Nash arrive. He hadn't looked happy to be here. And he hadn't even had that cup of beer when Mr. Dace drove up. He'd grabbed it up just before I realized Mr. Dace was here. As if he wanted to appear like he was enjoying himself.

"He's not lying," I heard myself say. "He got here just before you did."

All eyes turned to me. Mr. Dace frowned; then recognition came into his gaze. Then surprise. He hadn't expected to see me here. He didn't know me. We had only met today. But I guess I still didn't look like a girl who would be at a field party. Weight loss couldn't change it all for you. Inside you were the same.

"Talia?" Mr. Dace asked.

"Tallulah. Ta-loo-lah. Jesus what is it with teachers and her fucking name. It's not that hard to pronounce," Nash corrected him, clearly annoyed. It reminded me of a time when I thought he was my hero. I had worshiped him from afar. Clung to any smile or word he threw my way.

"I'm sorry. I just had Tallulah in my class this morning. I haven't memorized names yet." He didn't look at Nash as he said it. He looked at me.

"It's okay," I assured him.

"So you're still nice to him. You just went all bitch on me?" Nash asked. I ignored that.

"Jesus, Nash," Asa said, sounding frustrated.

Nash just laughed. There was no joy in his laugh. But there was pain. Didn't they all hear that? See it for what it was?

"We have workouts at seven in the morning. I want all of you at the field house at six. If you want to play Friday. Tallulah, I'll give you a ride home. Nash, you drive the others home. No one that has been drinking needs to drive."

"Tallulah came with me," Asa said before I could react.

"And have you been drinking?"

Asa sighed, then nodded.

"Then I am taking her home. The rest seemed to have cleared out." He looked around to see very few people standing around. "The party is over," he called out, then turned his attention back to Ryker. "You want to play? You'll make sure they all get home safely."

When he turned his head, his eyes met mine. "Let's go."

I didn't wait to argue. He was the adult after all. I glanced at Asa. "Bye" was all I knew to say.

"See you tomorrow," he replied.

Not being able to help myself, my eyes went to Nash. He smirked, then shook his head. "That's bullshit." I didn't know what he meant, and I didn't wait to find out. I followed Mr. Dace to his car. This night had turned out nothing like I had expected. In my head, I had built up this world they lived in, but the reality was much different. My life alone with my books was more appealing now I knew what this looked like.

You're All Fucking Shallow
CHAPTER 10

NASH

"You just gonna let him take her?" I asked Asa while watching Tallulah walk off with Coach fucking D. I'd seen the way he'd looked at her. I was sure most men looked at her that way. But that asshole was a teacher at her school, and she was seventeen years old.

Asa shrugged. "What else can I do? He's right. I've had a few beers. Can't have him calling my dad. Or her mom."

Weak. That excuse was weak. He was worried about the game. Getting to play. Not the fact Tallulah had gone off with a man ten years older than her. Hell, was I the only one who saw the man checking out her legs? It was pretty obvious.

"He isn't that stupid. He won't compromise the game," I replied, disgusted. This entire night shouldn't have happened. "Besides why did you bring her here? To a field party? She doesn't hang with this crowd."

Asa was the one who now looked annoyed. "Don't be an ass. She lost weight."

And he thought *I* was being an ass. "Wasn't talking about her weight. I was referring to her brain. She's studious. Doesn't party. Reads a lot. This isn't her scene."

"You don't know her scene. She was quiet and studious because she didn't have friends. She's a different person now. She's incredibly hot. Fun to talk to. Nice."

This conversation was annoying me with every word out of his mouth. I needed to drop it. But I didn't. "She's the same person. She was always all those things. She just looks different now. You're all fucking shallow."

Even as I said the words, I felt a twinge of guilt. Just because I'd spoken to her in the past didn't mean I had found her attractive. I hadn't been knocking at her door either. But at least I wasn't using her sudden outward appearance as the reason she is fun to talk to.

"How do you know? Until she showed up today, none of us knew her. I never saw you hanging around her before."

I wouldn't be thrown in the same disgusting clump as

them. I had been nice to her. "First grade. She sat three seats in front of me. Was nervous and shy. The teacher never pronounced her name correctly, and after a few times of correcting her and getting ignored, Tallulah stopped saying anything. I spoke up. Miss Barker got it right from then on. Third grade, she finished last in the one-mile run we did during PE. She was walking and breathing hard. None of you paid attention to the others laughing at her. Making jokes. I went over and told her she did great. I gave her my bottle of water since all of them were gone. Fourth grade, she fell and spilled her tray of food all over the cafeteria floor. While everyone laughed and said things like it was good she would miss a meal, I helped her up. Walked her to the bathroom so she could clean the red Jell-O off her shorts. Then gave her my tray of food—"

"Eleventh grade, I made a joke about her in a swimsuit, and you laughed. You laughed and never thought anything about it. Stop being so damn high and mighty. We are all the same. The girl was fat—we didn't notice her. She's thin now, and we are all looking." Ryker's interruption was like a slap in the face.

I let my memory go back. To that day. To the last day of school last year. It was one week before I decided to play football in Ryker's backyard with a bunch of friends and family members at the Memorial Day barbecue we had each year. The backyard game that would ruin everything for me. I didn't think about that. I thought about the week before. I saw Tallulah leaving school. Her arms full and a look of relief on her face. She was glad the year was over, just like us.

I spoke to her. It had never been a good-deed thing or a pity thing. I just liked her smile. Her eyes were so damn blue, and her smile was always real. It was also rare. But I could make her smile, and I liked it. I wanted to do it. Made me smile in return.

That day, though . . . after seeing her smile, my mind was right back on the date I had with Blakely that night and the sex I would be getting. I hadn't thought much more about Tallulah. Then Ryker . . . I paused and looked at him now. Studied his face. Let his words replay in my head. He'd made a joke about Tallulah in a bathing suit. No one needing to see that. Or something to that affect. I wasn't paying attention to him. My head was elsewhere.

But I laughed. Ryker laughed and I joined him.

Turning my head toward the line of trees Tallulah had long since walked through, it was like a brick wall had just slammed into my chest. She had heard him . . . us. He hadn't said it quietly. She had heard it.

She had heard me laugh.

My shoulders dropped, and I closed my eyes tightly. A pain squeezed my chest. Damn. I understood now. Her anger today. The words she almost said and didn't. She had heard Ryker make a joke at her expense. But I knew it wasn't the first time she'd heard a joke about her weight. We hadn't been the first people to laugh at her. So why was she so angry? Not at Ryker, but at me? Because I had been nice to her in the past?

That didn't seem fair. I should have been forgiven. I had good karma in my pocket to make up for the one mistake. The one stupid mistake I wish I could take back. It was done now, and I owed her an apology.

"Let's go," Ryker said then, breaking the silence.

"I didn't mean to laugh," I told him. Even though it made no difference to him either way.

He looked confused. "What?"

This conversation was pointless. "Nothing. I'll go put out the fire. Y'all get the garbage. You know we can't leave the field like this. Not if we expect to keep using it." Our grandfather would have both our asses if we did.

Ryker nodded and went to start cleaning. He barked at the others still standing around to help. I focused on making sure the blaze was out. I didn't like that Coach D had taken Tallulah home. Something was off there. It didn't seem as if he were doing it in a helpful way. Not when he was checking out her body. She was too damn naïve to even notice.

I doubted she'd ever been kissed. There was no way Asa had already made it that far with her. She may look different, but she was the same inside. Angry at me, sure. But now I knew why. I could fix that. I wanted to fix it. This was the first thing I wanted to do since I had gotten hurt.

Tallulah had a great smile. It made bad things seem less important. Like she saw a rainbow around the corner. Her eyes didn't twinkle with flirty intentions. She didn't even know how to do that. It was refreshing. I had enjoyed that about her. I missed it. I was going to make sure I got that smile again. I was done losing shit. I'd lost enough already.

Asa Griffith Doesn't Seem like Your Type

CHAPTER 11

TALLULAH

We got into Mr. Dace's car without speaking. I wasn't sure yet what to expect. If he was planning on telling my mother about the party or not. I didn't think it sounded very fair, considering I hadn't drunk anything. And I hadn't gotten in the car with a driver who had been drinking. Mom knew I was with Asa at Ryker's get-together to cheer Nash up.

That had been a massive fail. Nash had not been cheery at all. He looked miserable. And none of his friends seemed to understand why. That had to be frustrating him.

"Which way do I turn?" Mr. Dace asked.

"Left," I replied.

He turned his small car left and then glanced over at me again. "Asa Griffith doesn't seem like your type."

I'd just met the man. He had me for one class today. I frowned. "Why is that?" I asked, trying not to be snarky. I didn't want to make him an enemy and give him a reason to go talk to my mom.

He shrugged, turning his focus back to the road. "You seem more serious, mature, interested in your grades. Asa is a beast on the football field, but he's also not serious about anything else."

I had no reason not to be honest. "You're new. You don't know who I was. Or what I looked like before the summer. I've lost weight. A lot of weight. I didn't have many friends, or any friends before. A social life is new for me. I'm adjusting to it all."

"How did you lose weight?" he asked. That wasn't something the others had asked. They hadn't cared. They'd just liked the results.

"I walked daily. Drank water and ate healthy." I almost added that I did that all because I was angry, hurt, and bent on revenge. But I didn't.

"That's impressive. But you're right. I wasn't here last year. I didn't know you. What I saw was today. And the girl I noticed wasn't one to spend her Monday night at a party with drunk football players."

This was not his business. I didn't need life counseling from my English Literature teacher. "I take my grades seriously. I enjoy reading. But I can also have a social life."

He nodded. "Yes, you can. But you're just . . . more mature, or I assumed you were, than what I just witnessed back there. Those guys have years before they grow up."

I had never had a father. No man in my life to give me advice. Maybe this was normal. Older men liked to tell you what to expect from younger guys. I wasn't sure, so I tried not to get annoyed.

"What's your favorite book?" he asked.

"I don't have one favorite. I've got a bookshelf of favorites, though, and I doubt you've read any of them."

He smiled then. The corners of his mouth lifting as I glanced over at him. We came to the intersection that, if you followed straight ahead, would take you to the high school. "Turn right," I told him.

"I read too," he replied.

I didn't doubt that. He seemed the reading type. "I'm sure you do. But I know you don't read the books that are my favorites."

"And why's that?"

Leaning back, I finally relaxed since getting in this car. He was being much more pleasant now. "*Twilight*, Harry Potter all seven books, Beautiful Creatures, Hunger Games,

City of Bones, Matched, The Selection, *Before I Fall* . . ." I paused, grinning now. "Read any of those, Mr. Dace?"

He shot me a quick look, and his eyes were extra nice when he was smiling. I'd noticed that today in class. But in the moonlight they were almost . . . breathtaking. As was his smile. It was different. My stomach felt a little nervous.

"I've heard of several of them. Since many were made into movies. But keep in mind I've taught high school before. Those happen to be popular among many high school readers. And I did read the Hunger Games."

Out of all the books I mentioned, I wasn't surprised to hear that he'd read that series. "But not *Twilight*?" I teased.

He chuckled and shook his head. "No, that one didn't grab my interest."

"I can't imagine why," I drawled. Then I pointed up ahead. "The blue mailbox with the clouds painted on it. They . . . glow in the dark." I hated even having to explain that. I loved my mother, but she was whimsical. Silly. And she loved things that glowed in the dark.

"I see that. Makes it easy to spot." He seemed amused.

"Yes . . . I guess so."

He slowed before it was necessary, and although I was sure he was just being careful, I realized I wanted to believe it was because he was enjoying my company as much as I was his. "Do I need to come inside and explain my bringing you home to your parents?" he asked.

"No," I replied quickly.

"They won't see my car and wonder who I am?"

I knew my mom would be awake in the living room watching the news. But she wouldn't look outside. "It's just me and my mom. She trusts me. She has no reason not to. She knew where I was. I'll explain what happened and that you gave me a ride if she questions it. But she won't."

He looked surprised. "Very laid-back mother."

I gave a nod of agreement. "Yes. Who paints things to make them glow in the dark, bakes sweets that we don't eat, and decorates for Christmas the day after Halloween."

"Sounds like life with her is never dull."

"Not one moment." And I never could understand why the man who had supplied the sperm to make me hadn't stuck around. My mom was fun. She brought smiles and happiness just by being her. Why wouldn't a man want to be near that? He must have been a mean bastard. That's all I could figure.

"Where's your dad?" Mr. Dace asked.

"Don't have one of those," I replied flippantly, then reached for the door handle as the car came to a stop in my driveway.

"I'm sorry." He sounded like everyone did when I told

them I didn't have a father. Sad, concerned, like they wished they hadn't asked.

"Don't be. My life is good just like it is." I looked back at him before I got out of his car. "Thanks for the ride."

He studied me a moment. "You're welcome," he replied.

"See you in class," I added, then stepped out of the car.

"I look forward to it."

That comment made me pause. Just for a second. I closed the door behind me and walked to my front porch. His last five words teasing me. Like they meant something that I knew they didn't. But why had he said that? Why that way?

As I reached my front door, I glanced back to see him pull out of my drive. That was . . . very unexpected. All of it.

This Was the Smile I Missed Seeing
CHAPTER 12

NASH

Starting my day with my dad yelling at me to get my ass to school always made things feel brighter. Annoyed, I waited outside the school again, glad that the others had already gone inside. I wasn't in the mood to recap last night. Ryker had been furious with Coach D when I dropped him off at home. That wasn't going to have made for a pleasant workout this morning in the field house.

They'd all have been tired from their early morning and pissed because they had to be there. I hadn't climbed out of my vehicle yet when I saw a white Honda Civic pull up and park a few spots down. That was Tallulah's car and her parking spot. She'd been assigned it last year when she got her car. I suddenly had an interest in getting out and going inside.

By the time she was hurrying for the door, I had gotten close enough to catch up to her. Although I couldn't walk fast. I was closer to the entrance. "You're late," I said, just to get her attention.

She paused and turned to me. She'd been in such a hurry she hadn't noticed me until then. "Yeah and so are you," she replied.

"I've got a limp. Slows me down," I lied. I had simply not wanted to get out of bed this morning.

"Not that I have to explain myself to you, but my mother forgot about a cake she'd put in the oven, it caught on fire, and we had to put it out and get the smoke out of the house."

Okay her reason was more interesting. "Seriously?" I asked.

Tallulah rolled her eyes. "I wouldn't make that up."

Her dislike for me was getting to me, but that response made me laugh. It felt good to laugh. "Sounds like a fun morning."

She smirked as if she wanted to smile but wasn't going to. Not for me at least. "I smell like a fire. Not exactly thrilling."

She may have smelled like smoke, but she looked amazing. No makeup, her hair pulled up in a messy knot on her head, and she still stood out. Hard to miss. "Might keep the guys back so you can breathe today," I told her, knowing that wouldn't be the case.

"I guess I should consider that my silver lining," she snapped, annoyed.

She was enjoying this. She didn't want to enjoy it. That much was obvious. I didn't want her to hate me, but damn if it wasn't fun to hear her smart-ass comments. She was confident now. More sure of herself. The change in her was appealing. She had once tried to hide from the world. Blend in and hope no one noticed her. Now she held her head high and didn't back down. It was hard to walk away from, and I didn't want her to dislike me. Knowing I'd hurt her bothered me. As much fun as it was to see her roll her eyes at me and give me that annoyed smirk, I had to fix what I'd done. Or at least do the decent thing and apologize. She deserved that.

"I'm sorry." Even as I said it, I knew that words were weak, considering my actions.

Her confident smirk faded, and a confused frown took its place. She wasn't sure why I was apologizing. But I could see her mind working through it. I had to do better than just say I was sorry. She deserved more. An explanation.

"Last night I was reminded of something. Something I'm not proud of. Something I regret."

Understanding dawned in her gaze. She knew exactly

what I had done. It was why she'd been so angry with me. It had hurt her. My chest squeezed tighter, wishing I hadn't been so flippant. So careless. That moment I hadn't remembered had stuck with her.

"I wasn't really listening to Ryker that day. My head was elsewhere. I didn't think about it. I just reacted to his laughter with my own. It was thoughtless, cruel, and selfish. I should have said something to him, not just laughed. I was wrong. And I am sorry. I'm sorry for laughing. I'm sorry for not even remembering it happened. For being so damn wrapped up in my little world that I was blind to the others around me. How I was affecting them." I stopped. Saw her eyes soften. "How I was affecting you. I hurt you. I'll regret it forever. Please forgive me."

She didn't say anything right away. Instead she turned her head to stare off in another direction. I didn't push or say more. I let her process what I'd said. Decide if it was enough. If I was worth the forgiveness.

When she finally turned her head back to me, she gave me a small smile. Not the bright kind that I realized I'd once looked forward to. But one that was sincere in its own way. "You remember now, huh? Took you some time." Her words were laced with pain.

"I was an asshole. So was Ryker," I told her, wishing I could do more than just apologize.

"I'd never hated anyone before then. You were my first taste at hating someone. That hate drove me to walk every day. When I would have rather eaten a big piece of cake and read a book instead, I got up and walked because of you. I'd always depended on you to stand up for me. Speak to me. Notice me. I'd put you on some pedestal as perfect. Heroic. Truth was you were just a nice guy. Nothing more. You reacted the way the others always did, and it was crushing. But it changed me. I had the drive to lose the weight. Get healthier. I enjoy exercise now. And if you hadn't laughed, I'd still be that girl. I've spent months bitter, angry, bent on revenge. But now . . . I don't feel any of that. Seeing you and realizing I let your actions have so much power over me was my fault. I shouldn't have given you that power. Thanks for the apology, but it's irrelevant now and a little late."

There was no softness, no forgiveness in her voice. Knowing my laughter had affected her like that made me feel even worse. "Is that what you were talking about yesterday? Why you started walking?" A simple nod of her head confirmed what I'd already figured out. "I wish your hurt because of my actions hadn't been why you did it."

She lifted a corner of her mouth as if that amused her. "Hate, Nash. It was hate."

Although she wanted me to believe she no longer cared,

that she had moved on and forgotten it, the tone of her voice told me otherwise. She may not have hated me anymore, but she didn't like me. And I wanted to fix that. Not just to ease my guilt, but because I wanted to get to know the girl she'd become.

The late bell rang, and we heard it echo outside.

"Now we're really late," she said, trying not to look worried.

I shrugged. Not a big deal. "We won't miss much."

"Maybe, but I'm never late."

"Never hurts to try something new," I replied.

Tallulah shot me an annoyed glare. "Yeah, well, that road isn't one I plan on going down. I'll try new things that don't affect my grades and college acceptance letters."

Jesus she was serious. And it was sexy as hell. "Lighten up, girl. It's just one tardy."

Tallulah rolled her eyes at me yet again and hurried on toward the entrance. I watched her go, enjoying the view in those shorts she was wearing. I followed behind her, slower simply because I couldn't move that fast anymore. The office would only let me be late so many times before they stopped being understanding.

She was fast, because when I got to the office, Tallulah was already gone. Mrs. Murphy was too busy getting everyone checked in to have a tardy slip prepared for me already. There were three other people in front of me. That was odd. No one else was outside. They had to have been here before she got in here. How had she gotten her tardy slip and already gone to class?

I glanced around to see if she was anywhere, but nothing. When it was my turn to sign in, I noticed her name wasn't on the tardy sheet. "Tallulah Liddell just came in. Did she not check in?" I asked Mrs. Murphy.

She slid my slip across the counter to me. "She did come in, but Mr. Dace was in the hallway and said he had her excuse. She'd been helping him with something. Now don't make this tardy thing a habit, Nash." Then she turned to the student behind me.

Coach D again . . . I didn't trust that man.

The Teacher Will Be Looking for You
CHAPTER 13

TALLULAH

I wasn't a good liar. I didn't like to lie. This felt like a lie. Mr. Dace saving me from getting my first tardy ever. I was late. Just like the others in the office waiting to get a tardy slip. But I had gone with him. The other option would have been to call my teacher a liar in front of everyone and refuse. It had caught me by surprise, and thinking fast wasn't my strong suit. I needed time to weigh my options and make a decision.

Asa found me after third period. He was all flirty smiles and confidence. "Last night didn't end the way I wanted it to," he said, grinning at me.

I wasn't sure it had ended the way I wanted it to either.

I was very conflicted about that. I liked Mr. Dace. He was nice, smart, and handsome, and that last one was the issue. He was handsome. Distractingly so. It wasn't a good idea for me to develop a crush on my teacher. And I was afraid that was a possibility.

"It was definitely an interesting end to the evening," I replied, not knowing what else to say.

"Coach D is young and doesn't know how we do things around here."

"He was doing his job." I defended him before I had time to think about it.

Asa shrugged. "I guess. You going to the game Friday night?" He changed the subject that easily.

The truth was I had never been to a football game. I knew I should go. This was my senior year. I wanted to experience high school. All that I had missed out on by being a recluse. I wanted no regrets when I looked back. "Yes," I told him. Although I wasn't sure with who.

"After the game, meet me on the field. We'll go to the field party together. There should be no interruptions on a Friday night," he said with a roll of his eyes as if Mr. Dace was ridiculous.

"Um, I don't know—" I was cut off from having to turn down his offer.

"Not tardy, huh?" Nash's voice came from behind me.

I paused, and the guilt of my morning lie was back. Only Nash would know the truth. I had been with him when the late bell rang. Taking a deep breath, I turned to meet his gaze.

"That wasn't my idea. He surprised me. I didn't . . . I didn't know what to say."

Nash smirked. "You say nothing. Be glad you didn't have to wait in that line."

He'd waited in line. I didn't want to care about that. I wanted to be tough and jaded where he was concerned. But it wasn't fair that I didn't have to get marked as tardy. I should have said something to Mr. Dace.

"I should have, though. It's not honest," I admitted.

"What's not honest?" Asa asked, reminding me he was there.

Nash glanced over my shoulder toward Asa. "Nothing. I'm just giving Miss Goody-Goody here a hard time." He wasn't telling Asa about it. Not that I'd done something terribly wrong. I was making more out of this than there really was.

"Were you late?" Asa asked me.

I opened my mouth to speak, but Nash beat me to it. "No. She got in before the bell. I'm slow. I didn't make it."

Hearing him lie for me made this worse.

"It was a hectic morning," I explained.

"Burning stoves can stress one out," Nash agreed.

"Whose stove was burning?" Asa asked.

I glanced back at Asa. "My mother forgot about a cake in the oven. It caught on fire."

Asa's eyebrows shot up. "Damn."

"I've got to get to English Lit," I told both of them. I didn't want to be late to Mr. Dace's class. Or any class ever again.

"Better get to that one. The teacher will be looking for you," Nash drawled. His tone made me feel uncomfortable. Like I needed to defend myself. My cheeks felt warm, and that just made me angry.

"Bye," I muttered at both of them without looking in either direction, then hurried away into the crowded hallway. Was it obvious that I had a bit of a crush on Mr. Dace? Is that what Nash was saying? I hadn't said or done anything to warrant that. He was attractive and young. I would guess most of the girls had a crush on him. It wasn't like I was going to start writing him love letters and leaving them on his desk.

I reached his classroom door five minutes before the bell. I hadn't even been close to being late. There was no one inside yet. No one but Mr. Dace. Now I looked stalkerish. Frowning, I blamed this on Nash. He'd made me concerned about something stupid. I was always early for my classes. I didn't socialize in the hallways. My being at Literature early was normal for me. Expected.

"Tallulah," Mr. Dace said, smiling as I walked into his room and his eyes met mine. He appeared pleased I was on time. Not creeped out. I was going to ignore Nash's comment and relax. I liked this class. Mr. Dace was a good teacher. At least based on the one class I had with him yesterday, he was good.

"How has your morning been?" he asked, putting down the book in his hands and giving me his complete attention.

"Good, and yours?"

The corner of his mouth lifted. "It's getting better."

The way he said it made me pause. It was almost . . . No. I was being silly. Mr. Dace did not mean it the way I took it. "Oh, well, that's good," I replied, realizing I had just said *good* in my last response. I was nervous with him. I couldn't relax.

"Hello, Mr. Dace," Bianca Valley said as she entered the room. Her shirt tight and her cleavage about to spill out of the top. She tossed her long black hair over her shoulder and batted her lashes at him. That was what I did not want to appear like to him.

"Good morning," he replied with a smile that wasn't at all flirty. He then turned his gaze back to me. Most males didn't look away from Bianca's shirts. Her chest size was impressive. I had to give it to him. He was a classy guy.

"I've got a book I think you'll enjoy. It's not your norm, but I found it last night on my shelf, and I believe it's one that will keep your interest."

"Oh, okay," I replied, trying not to look shocked that he had thought about me enough to pick me out a book.

"I've been wondering," Bianca said as she perched herself on the edge of his desk. "How old are you exactly? You don't look much older than me." She leaned toward him, and I dropped my gaze to my notebook on my desk.

"That's not relevant to this class." His chair moved, and I lifted my eyes to see him stand up and put distance between them. "Sitting on my desk is also considered inappropriate. There are plenty of desks available in the room." He turned his back to her then and started preparing for the others to arrive. I watched him a moment, surprised by how he had dealt with Bianca. Most male teachers forgot that anyone else was in the room when she chose to flirt with them.

Mr. Dace was different.

CHAPTER 14

NASH

I was waiting on her. Tallulah. I was outside waiting on her. I just needed to admit that to myself and deal with it. The past two days, she'd been hard to catch in the halls. I'd barely seen her. She hadn't been on Asa's arm like he wanted, and during lunch she was nowhere to be found. I tried not to make it obvious I was looking for her. Asa was less obvious. He'd asked around and would openly watch for her everywhere.

The only glimpse I'd seen of her today was when she'd walked out of the library and gone in the opposite direction of me. Her avoiding me I didn't like. I could deal with her smart mouth and anger as long as I got to see her and talk to her. It was Friday, and tonight was the first game. I didn't want to be there. But the guys all expected me to be.

Standing on the sidelines while I watched them all live my senior dream wasn't exactly going to be easy. I had battled with it all damn day. Ryker fully believed I would be there on the field with him. He didn't question it.

My dad assumed I'd be there "supporting the team" and all that shit. I'd played ball with these guys since I was in elementary school. We had started this thing together, and I was expected to end it together. But I wouldn't be playing. None of them seemed to care about that, though. They didn't get how hard that was going to be.

Tallulah appeared in the front doors of the building. The breeze caught her long blond hair, and it reminded me of a commercial. One of those shampoo commercials where the girls are hot and their hair is perfect.

Her head turned, and her eyes didn't seem to dwell on anything or anyone in particular. It was as if she were out here all alone, not noticing her surroundings. The attention she was getting from guys, and girls for that matter. She was hard not to look at. One would assume that she was enjoying the attention. Soaking it in and letting everyone bask in her beauty. Ignoring them all while walking through the parking lot knowing all eyes were on her.

But that wasn't the case. This was Tallulah. I saw it for

what it really was. She still carried herself and acted like she had for the past eleven years. She didn't want to draw attention. She was afraid of being made fun of. This was how she had gone around unnoticed. Ignored. Problem was, no one was ignoring her now. They were unable to look away.

I had always noticed her. Sure, she had always had a pretty face. But that hadn't been why. I liked her smile, the way she didn't try to get attention, how smart she was. I liked hearing her laugh. She was genuine. It was rare.

I was standing near her car and waited until she got closer before walking over to stand beside it. Her gaze found me. She paused a second, then continued toward me. I didn't get a smile, which was a shame. I really liked her smile. A whole damn lot. Instead, I got an irritated scowl.

She stopped as she reached me. "Why are you at my car?"

"You've been hard to find," I told her.

She did a small shrug of her shoulders. "Trying to keep up with the advanced classes. The library is my friend. You aren't. Now if you'll excuse me, I need to go."

I wondered if she'd been spending any extra time with Coach D, but I didn't ask. I knew her well enough to know she wouldn't get it. She was too naïve to see what the man was doing. I wasn't, though. And I was watching. Someone had to look out for her.

"Maybe I should try out the library more often. Could only help my grades," I replied.

Her eyes widened as if the idea made her nervous, but she recovered quickly. "I'm sure it would. I need to go."

This verbal battle was fun, but I wanted her to smile at me, dammit. She liked this too. She didn't act like it, but there was something there. An energy between us. And it wasn't just the anger she was still clinging to. When the words *go out with me tonight* came pouring from my mouth, I was as surprised as she was.

Her eyes went wide, and her perfect pink mouth made a small O shape. As if that had been the last thing she expected me to ask. I had wanted it, but the words just coming out like that hadn't been the smoothest way of asking. I was losing my edge.

"The game is tonight," she said after blinking away her surprise. No smart-ass comment this time. I'd thrown a curveball at her, and she hadn't been ready.

I nodded. "It is. I am expected to stand on the sidelines. It's the last thing I want to do, yet I can't imagine not being there. If you came . . . if you were in the stands waiting on me . . . it would make it a hell of a lot easier." And that was the truth.

"Why me? I don't like you. I can't imagine I'd make your night better." Her words were meant to sound harsh, but it seemed she was losing her edge too. Her voice had quavered nervously. I bit back a grin.

"Because you're the only person in this town that doesn't feel sorry for me." As I said it, I realized that was part of it. My attraction to her.

She took a deep breath and stared off toward the field. Her lips pursed in a distasteful pucker. Like she didn't want to respond to this. If it wasn't so damn cute, I'd be insulted. I'd never had a girl this pissed off that I'd asked her out before. When she finally swung her gaze back to me, she sighed.

"Okay." She said that one word as if it was the hardest thing she'd ever said. There was no pleasure in her tone or her expression. She didn't like saying yes. But I didn't care, because that one word made tonight and all the other shit in my life seem easier. Less painful. My chest felt light, and I was excited. It had been so long since I had been excited about anything.

"Really?" I asked, grinning like an idiot.

I watched as she fought back a smile to keep her annoyed glare in place. She was struggling, and I only grinned harder.

"I don't have to be here for warmups. I'll pick you up at six thirty. We can grab a burger before the game. Then after we can go wherever you want. The field, to get more food, a movie."

"Fine," she said. No excitement there, but I had enough for the both of us. She wanted to hate me still, but she didn't. I could break through that wall. Or I'd go down trying at least.

"Tallulah," a male voice called out, and my skin crawled. She jerked her head toward Coach D as he walked toward us. He was acting like the teacher he was supposed to be, but I could see from the way he was glaring in my direction that his head was elsewhere.

"Yes, Mr. Dace?" she asked, her voice suddenly nervous. Unsure.

"The office was supposed to call you up earlier to tell you that your application for teacher's aid was accepted. They've assigned you to me during your last period, and you receive extra credit if you arrive an hour early in the morning."

I stood there wanting to put my fist between that horny bastard's eyes. I was unable to if I wanted to stay in school. And what was the office thinking? She was a beautiful teenage girl, and he was a young male teacher. They should have put her with a woman teacher.

"Oh, okay. Did you need me today? I didn't know."

He acted as if I wasn't even standing there. Didn't acknowledge my existence. "I've got to get ready for the game. Just be there at seven on Monday morning. I'll go over all I need you to do this semester. Enjoy your weekend." He then glanced at me. "I'll see you on the field tonight." That was his way of telling me I had to be there. Who the fuck did he think he was? He was never my coach. He didn't tell me what I was going to do. If I was on that field tonight, it would be because I wanted to be. Not because he told me to be.

I didn't respond to him. I wanted him to know I saw it. I knew what he was doing. That this thing with Tallulah wasn't going to be overlooked. If he stepped out of line, I'd make sure it never happened again. She was trusting and innocent. He saw that.

"Good luck tonight," Tallulah said, her smile more nervous than when she looked at me.

He grinned. It wasn't the kind a teacher gives a student. "Thanks. You better be there."

She turned her head to look at me, and her smile wavered. "I will be."

I wanted her to say we had a date. Something. Just to piss him off and remind him she was seventeen years old. She held my gaze. There was something unsaid in that moment. She didn't want his attention. After a moment of awkward silence, Coach D walked off, and she didn't watch him go.

Score one for me.

This Was Not Disney World
CHAPTER 15

TALLULAH

You know those daydreams you have for years . . . the ones you know won't come true, but they get you through the day? The kind I shouldn't have been having about Nash. The excitement I shouldn't have felt but did. Instead of dreading my date with Nash, I was in a state of giddiness. All I could do was smile, feel wistful. The reality was it was hard to turn off years of those dreams. To forget them. Those little fantasies are what kept me going when no one spoke to me in the hallways. When I heard girls giggling about my weight or clothing. They were my escape.

However, not one single time while I was in my little bubble of imagination did I truly believe it would come true. I knew it was just that, a dream. And this was not Disney World. Dreams did not come true. It was high school, and it sucked. Living in my head and my wistful thoughts was fine since I had that firm grasp on reality.

The past three hours, I had changed my clothes seven times. Washed my hair and restyled it three times and had to fight the urge to chew off all my nails. Not bite. Chew those bad boys completely off to the skin. I was a nervous wreck. In my head, it hadn't been this way. I had been charming and lovely. My clothes had been perfect. I had been confident and full of self-worth. But here in the real world, I felt like I might throw up.

Girls didn't get to experience their daydreams. That only happened in cheesy movies that didn't depict high school properly at all. For example, if a girl is wearing a designer skirt that shows off her bottom when she walks, and her boobs are hanging out of her shirt while she flashes skin on her stomach, then she is not in a real high school. Only in TV land can that happen. Just like only in TV land does a girl's crush who is way out of her league ask her out.

But here I was. Getting ready for a date with Nash Lee. When he had asked me, it had taken all my focus not to grab on to my car for support. My knees went weak, my stomach was so tied up in knots I thought I needed to bend at the waist, and I couldn't remember how to use words.

Luckily, Mr. Dace arrived and snapped me out of my shock. Given me a moment to process it all. I owed him one for perfect timing.

Asa taking me to a field party, Ryker flirting with me, other guys winking and smiling at me in the hallways had all been fine. I had adjusted to no longer being ignored. It still surprised me, but I wasn't swooning over it. I'd been so angry with Nash that I had been riding on that hate and assumed I'd be immune to him. Or I would at least be able to focus my energy toward him differently. But then he apologized. It wasn't enough. That apology. But my dang silly heart felt something. Why was it so hard to still hate him? He'd hurt me. He'd been cruel.

The truth was deep down I had forgiven him. I just didn't want to. There was damage there he'd caused. Even if he made my heart flutter, he didn't have to know. He didn't deserve to know.

I didn't care if he limped. I didn't care if he played football. I didn't care if he started sitting in the library to read during lunch and became a recluse. None of those things would change how I felt about him. It was never his popularity that I was attracted to. It was his heart. He had been kind when others hadn't. I'd loved him silently. His laughter at Ryker's words, though, still rang in my memory.

"Have you decided on an outfit yet?" Mom asked from

my open bedroom door. I turned to see her with a glass of red wine in her hands and a smile on her face. She was entirely too excited about this. She knew my feelings for Nash. They had been hard to hide from my one friend in life. She was my mother. She corrected me, expected the best out of me, and didn't let me get away with talking back or being disrespectful. She was also my best friend.

"I think," I replied, holding out my hands and turning in a circle. After trying on everything new in my closet, I had come back to the very first thing I had pulled out. A blue-jean skirt that hit midthigh and a T-shirt that had been bought with the worn look and a cut-out triangle on the chest, giving it a V shape yet keeping the neckline there. The faded blue made my eyes pop, and the word *Dreamer* on the front was perfect. Especially for tonight. I pointed at my boots. "It's between either those or the wedges. I thought the boots may be easier if we end up at the field party."

Mom looked like a giddy teenager with her grin. "Boots definitely. They go perfect with that look. Very edgy, sexy, casual. I like it. I may steal it."

I shook my head. "No. You are not wearing this."

She put a hand on her narrow hip and cocked an eyebrow at me. "Are you insinuating I am too old to wear that?"

"No, but you'll look better in it. I don't need my mom outdoing me," I replied honestly.

She didn't like that. Her smile turned into a frown. "You are kidding me, right? Tallulah, honey, you're stunning. Young and beautiful inside and out. You always have been. No matter what size you are, you are a beauty who also happens to be the best part of me. You're my one great achievement in life. You are what I am proud of most in this world. Don't you ever believe that you are less than. You hold your head high."

I held up my hand to stop her or she'd keep going, and I would never be ready in time. "Mom, okay. I know you love me. I shouldn't have said that. You can wear any of my clothes. Everyone always mistakes us for sisters anyway. I have good genes. I should be thankful. I am thankful."

She started to smile again. "You're nervous. Don't be. Nash Lee is the lucky one. You go out with him tonight and know he is who should be nervous. He has you on his arm."

I rolled my eyes. My mother was a bigger dreamer than me. "Says my mother and biggest fan. It's Nash. He's not nervous. He has never been the fat kid who tried to blend in with the walls."

"Tallulah," she started again, and I hurried in to stop her.

"Mom, I'm kidding. Just let me get ready. I'm going to

be nervous. Nash has been my crush since I started school here. It's unavoidable. I am going to be nervous."

She sighed, then shrugged. "Okay. Fine. Get ready. But look at yourself in that mirror good." She started to turn to leave, then flashed me one last smile. "I love you."

"I love you, too."

Finally I was alone again.

I took in my body in the mirror. The way I fit into clothing now. I still felt the same inside. Seeing my outward appearance didn't change more than my clothing size. Confidence didn't come from the way you could or could not wear a short skirt. It came from inside.

"You're a good person. You're smart. The way you look isn't who you are," I whispered to the girl in the mirror. She was still so new to me. I didn't recognize myself when I saw my reflection. It always took me a second to remember that was me now.

Although my reflection couldn't respond, I nodded for her. Then smiled because I was being extremely dramatic. I had thirty minutes left to get on my boots and decide if my hair was going up or down.

Was I That Damn Shallow?

CHAPTER 16

NASH

The two-story white house had been on my road all my life. Every Halloween it was decorated the best. When I was a kid, it was my favorite house to trick-or-treat at. Each Christmas the lights from this house outdid everyone else on the street. I passed the house during those holidays and always glanced its way to see what new things had been added.

The one thing I never thought about was that this was Tallulah's house. I liked the decorations, but the people who lived here hadn't been something I gave much thought to. I parked my just-washed Escalade in the driveway and got out. I was self-conscious of my limp. My mind immediately went to Tallulah watching me from one of the windows on the second floor and seeing the way I walked. I hated this feeling, knowing that I was different.

Being nervous about a date wasn't something I was familiar with. That had changed too. I couldn't walk as fast. People noticed my limp and watched me. I sure as hell didn't have a swagger anymore. I glanced back at my car and thought about leaving, forgetting this. I was more than likely a pity date. Of all the girls at Lawton High, she would be the one to go out with a guy because she felt sorry for him. She knew what it was like to be unwanted.

But I had never stood a girl up, and I wasn't about to start now. Walking to her door, I silently prayed she wasn't watching me walk. Didn't have to be reminded what she was going out with tonight. I shouldn't have asked her, but I did. I had wanted to, and she'd said yes so easily.

The front door wasn't covered in decorations. It was the end of August, and the holidays that Tallulah's mother seemed to love hadn't begun yet. I rang the doorbell and waited. But only for a moment.

The door swung open, and the attractive petite woman who I remembered giving me candy as a child stood there smiling. Tallulah had never come to school events. Her mother wasn't one who was in the PTA or any other parent organization. I never realized this was her house.

"Nash," she said brightly. "It's nice to see you. Come on in. Tallulah is almost ready."

She knew me. Which made it even more embarrassing that I didn't know if her last name was the same as Tallulah's. I didn't know her first name either. I had no name to refer to her by. I slapped on a smile. "No hurry. I'm maybe a few minutes early." I wasn't. But it sounded good to say it.

Her mother stepped back and waved me inside. The entry was small and led right into a large living area. Everything was bright and cheery. Very different. Interesting artwork and a ceiling painted the blue of the sky were the first things to catch my attention. There were even a few clouds up there.

"I like the sky, and I like to paint. It's my thing," her mother explained. I glanced over at her, and she was also looking up at the ceiling, smiling with a fondness. "Took me a month to paint that thing. I'm scared of heights you see, so this was a challenge. But I did a little every day. Now I can relax and enjoy it any time I want."

Was Tallulah this much of a dreamer? She didn't appear to be. I would guess it was hard to ever be negative in this kind of home. Her mother didn't seem to be the kind who was ever negative.

"It's cool," I agreed. Because it was.

"Let me show you the kitchen!" she said with obvious

pride in her voice. I followed as she led me to the next room. It was blue. Everything was a different shade of blue. "Look up."

I did as told, and it took me a moment, but I figured it out. We were under the sea. I glanced back down after looking up at the world from under the water to notice a few pieces of sea life here and there. This would be one hard house to sell because, as creative as all this was, it would take someone like Tallulah's mom to appreciate it. My mother for example . . . this would not be her thing.

"I'm ready. I'll rescue you before she takes you to the staircase to show you the ceiling there."

I turned to Tallulah, and the wildly painted house was forgotten. Tallulah was stunning. Breathtaking. No wonder the twenty-seven-year-old teacher was attracted to her. She didn't look seventeen. Dressed like this, she looked older. When everyone saw her tonight, she'd have plenty of guys to choose from. This was possibly the only date I'd get. The sympathy date would be done.

"The bathroom looks like the night sky, her bedroom looks like a stormy sky, and the stairs look like you're under the stairs in the cupboard with Harry Potter." Tallulah smirked. "I went through a Harry Potter stage when I was younger, and she did it for my birthday surprise." Then she turned to her mother. "Thanks for keeping him entertained.

Love you," she said, then hugged her mom, who kissed her on the cheek.

"Love you. Have fun," she said to me as well as Tallulah. "Drive careful. Wear your seat belts." My mother always said the same thing when I left the house.

"Always," Tallulah replied. Then she turned back to me, and her smile faded. She wasn't full of confidence. She wasn't trying to be flirty. There wasn't the "aren't I gorgeous" smirk on her lips. I raised an eyebrow as if to challenge her. Would she really say something rude right here in front of her mother? I loved our verbal combat, but I doubted she'd start it up in front of her eager mother. Then it happened. She smiled. At me. I'd missed that smile. Really missed it. It was slow and a little shy. That was what made her smile so damn beautiful. It wasn't arrogant. It was unique, something I had only experienced with Tallulah. I didn't want that to change. I didn't want her to change.

Why hadn't I asked her out before? I'd always loved her smile. It made me feel good. Why had I waited until she was thin? Was I that damn shallow?

Yes.

I was.

And I didn't like to admit it. Or accept it. But I was.

"You look beautiful," I told her, not caring that her mother was still standing there.

Her cheeks turned a pretty pink, and she lowered her lashes, unable to look at me as she said, "Thank you."

That was what I'd been missing. Now that I realized it was out there. The guilt from not asking her out before her weight loss was heavy. Made me feel superficial. When Tallulah was anything but. She was spending her first Friday night back at high school with me. A cripple. Who she wanted to hate. I'd hurt her and caused pain that she was trying like hell to hold against me. But she was crumbling. Right before my eyes.

"Let's go get a burger," I said when it was obvious she was embarrassed by my compliment and unsure how to handle it. She hadn't received many of those in her life. The way she accepted it was so damn sweet.

"Okay," she agreed, peeking back up at me.

"Bye, y'all," her mother called out.

"It was nice to officially meet you," I told her mother.

She beamed brightly and Tallulah turned and we walked out of the house.

When the door closed behind us, she looked at me and said, "I promise she's not crazy."

I laughed. Because I hadn't been thinking that at all. But the serious expression on Tallulah's face was adorable. My chest was light. I was happy.

Damn.

There Is a Lot You Don't
Know about Me

CHAPTER 17

TALLULAH

"Are you scared of heights like your mom?"

I thought that was an odd question. It was the first thing he asked when we got in his vehicle. I'd been a little distracted thinking that I was sitting in Nash Lee's famous silver Escalade. Girls had wanted to be in this Escalade since the moment he'd driven it into the parking lot the first time at school. A lot had been whispered to have happened in the back of this Escalade as well. But the question about my fear of heights snapped me back to the moment. Away from my thoughts.

"No. That's my mom's issue. Not mine."

He flashed me a grin. "Good." Then he didn't say any more about it. The next thing he asked was "Are your parents divorced?"

I shook my head. "They were never married. I've never met my dad. Don't care to."

He frowned. "Sounds like a douche."

I nodded my head in agreement. "I can't imagine what my mother ever saw in him. Unless he charmed her. She's easily charmed. Lives in a happy place where bad things don't happen. Even when they do, she finds the bright side and carries on."

When I was younger, that had annoyed me about my mom. I wanted her to accept reality. I didn't understand why she didn't get upset about bad things. Like the time we had to go a month on peanut butter sandwiches and milk because our car had broken down and to fix it cost most of her monthly paycheck. But instead of being upset, she'd cut the sandwiches in funny shapes. Made a new story out of the sandwich characters every night. It was just how she was. Always optimistic. I understood that as I got older. And now I was thankful for it. She'd kept me smiling many times when I just wanted to cry.

"I always loved trick-or-treating at your house the best. Your mom had the best decorations and homemade treats.

Those cupcakes were more exciting than any candy. And one year it was Rice Krispies treats shaped like pumpkins. A kid's jackpot."

I smiled. Mom always loved Halloween and Christmas. She made both those holidays big. Her excitement over them made me equally excited. It wouldn't be but a few more weeks before she'd have me crawl into the attic and hand her down the Halloween decorations. She may have painted the ceilings, but she still wouldn't climb the attic ladder. That was my job.

"We spent days before Halloween making those. You should see what all she makes for Christmas. My teachers look forward to the large holiday tins full of treats she brings up to the school. It was embarrassing when she kept doing it once I got to junior high school, but I got over it. Now I don't make a fuss when I have to haul all those tins to the school and hand them out."

Nash chuckled. "Damn, she's like Martha Stewart."

"Not even close! Martha cleans her house a lot more often than my mom."

Nash was still grinning when he pulled into the burger place in town. "I called in our order. Wait here. I'll go grab it."

I nodded, confused. Why weren't we eating in there? My first thought was he was embarrassed to be seen with me. I almost expected that. But then I figured that couldn't be it. He was taking me to the football game and out afterward. I tried not to let the old Tallulah leak through. The self-conscious one. The girl who tried to hide from everyone so no one would make fun of her.

Blakely was walking out with a group of cheerleaders. They were all dressed for the game. I knew they hadn't actually eaten in there. Not before they cheered for hours on the field. But several had to-go cups of coffee or soda. Blakely was looking back inside, and she sighed dramatically, then said something to the other girls. I couldn't be sure, but it looked like she was talking about Nash. Almost as if she felt sorry for him. Or pitied him.

When he walked out, she said something to him, and he paused. His entire body tensed, and I reacted before I could think it through. Opening the door to his Escalade, I stepped out. I was almost to the group before the other girls started to notice me. I'd never tried to actually strut. Until now. I held my head high. Put on a confident face and slung my hair back over my left shoulder.

I had seen this done hundreds of times by the very group of girls I was about to approach. Drawing attention to myself like this made me want to puke. But I didn't let that show. I acted as if I owned the world and it was amusing.

"You found friends," I said to Nash as I slipped an arm around his free one and stood there beside him. "Aren't y'all gonna be late?" I asked as sweetly as I could, keeping my eyes on Blakely.

She looked confused and surprised.

"Are you with her?" Blakely finally asked, her face turning from the pity she had to a pinched, angry look.

"Tallulah, this is Blakely. I'm sure you've never met her. She's very self-absorbed. Doesn't make friends easily," Nash said with ease. Not missing a beat. I felt like giving him a high five.

"I know who she is!" Blakely snapped. "Everybody knows about the fat girl who lost weight. Freak." She said the words in hopes of hurting me. But I had spent years watching people quietly from the corner. I could read expressions better than most. She was jealous. She had left Nash but hadn't expected him to move on so easily or quickly. It was hurting her ego.

"I was unaware that weight loss was freakish. You've enlightened me," I replied with a smile.

She started to say something else to me but snapped her mouth shut, then swung her gaze back to Nash. "We broke up, what? Three days ago? And you're already out with someone?" She sounded outraged. Was this girl for real? I had seen her with Hunter since Monday.

"Oh, y'all just broke up on Tuesday? Was Hunter aware of that? Because the groping session that was going on in the hallway during second period Monday between the two of you made it seem you were perfectly available."

Her eyes widened then went to slits as she glared at me. "Stay out of this, bitch! No one asked for your fucking opinion."

Nash moved then. He stood between us in a protective move. "Don't speak to her like that. In fact, Blakely, if you could not speak to me at all, that would be best." He turned and took my hand. "Let's go. She's a waste of our time."

I couldn't help but glance back over my shoulder as we walked to his Escalade and flash her a smile.

"BITCH!" she yelled at me.

"Are you taunting her?" Nash asked me with a trace of humor in his tone.

"Probably," I admitted.

"You're a little spitfire, Miss Liddell. I never knew."

I shrugged as he opened the passenger door for me. "There is a lot you don't know about me."

He was still watching me after I climbed in and sat down. "I'd like to change that."

The smile that spread across my face was so big it almost hurt. Almost.

My Life and Criminal Record
Are in Your Hands

CHAPTER 18

NASH

The water tower was a place I hadn't gone in years. You could see the football field from here. I used to watch the older guys play from this spot and dream of the day I could play. Since I had been on that field, I hadn't been back here.

"Nash," Tallulah said hesitantly as she stared at the water tower in front of us. I opened my door to climb out with the dinner I'd gotten us in my hand.

"Grab the waters. I'll stick them in my pockets," I said, then got out.

She didn't follow immediately. I grinned as I waited for her to join me. When she finally got out of the Escalade, she had the bottles in her hand, and a frown wrinkled the space between her eyebrows. "Are we . . . are we going up that?" she asked, looking up at the water tower.

"I thought you said you weren't scared of heights," I reminded her, enjoying this. Seeing her battle with herself over doing this.

"Heights I'm not scared of . . . however, the police I would rather not piss off."

That made me chuckle. "The cops won't come after us."

She didn't look convinced. "Climbing the water tower is illegal."

"Technically, yes. But all the cops in town are already at the football field. Probably all having a burger, fries, and some nachos compliments of the Booster Club. None of them are worried about teens climbing water towers."

With a sigh, she nodded. "Okay. Let's do this."

That was easy. "You go first. I'll come up behind you in case you slip."

She shot me an annoyed glare. "Not a comforting thought."

"What? I might have a limp, but I haven't lost the strength in these bad boys," I said, flexing my arms.

She laughed, and the tension in her eyes faded. "My life and criminal record are in your hands."

"Noted."

She walked toward the tower. Still hesitant in her steps,

but she was doing it. As a kid, I never considered the cops or danger of this. It was just my quiet place to dream. A dream that was now gone. I gave my head a hard shake. I wasn't going to think about that. Not now. I would later, while on the field, as I watched my teammates play the first game of our senior year. My former teammates.

Tallulah came to the bottom of the ladder, and she tilted her head back to look up. The way her wavy blond hair blew gently in the breeze. Her waist small but her hips flared just enough. She wasn't too thin. I liked that. She had curves. She also knew how to dress her curves. Tonight wasn't going to be easy for me. But being with her made it better. Easier. She didn't know that. Maybe I'd tell her. Maybe I wouldn't. Maybe I'd just enjoy this. Be thankful she was here, that she forgave me.

"Should I take off these boots? Seems like it would be hard to climb this with boots."

I hadn't thought of that, but she had a point. Barefoot would be better. "Yeah. Go barefoot. It'll be easier."

She bent down and slipped a foot out of each boot, then stood back up and gave me a small grin before turning back to the ladder. Our burgers were going to get cold by the time we got up there with all these delays. Not that I cared. I was enjoying myself.

"Okay, here I go," she announced without looking back.

"I'm right behind you," I assured her.

"You better be. If I get arrested, you are going with me."

"Would make for a great story at school on Monday."

She laughed loudly. That sound. It always made me smile.

Climbing up the tower, I tried to stay focused on making sure she was steady. Be alert. But she was wearing a skirt. It was hard not to look up. I was fighting it.

"Are you looking up my skirt?" she called down to me as if she could read my thoughts.

"No. I thought about it. Considered it, but I'm being a gentleman. It's a rare thing. Make a note of it."

"I'll be sure to put it in my diary," she shot back.

It was the longest amount of time I had ever taken to climb the tower. But we made it finally. Tallulah went to the railing and stared out at the town beneath us. It was a view most people never saw of Lawton. "You can see the field so good from here," she said when her gaze landed on our school.

"Yeah," I agreed, not saying anything more. I had come up here to face this without my friends watching me first. To deal with the fact I'm not on that field tonight warming up. But knowing Tallulah was here to observe me suddenly made me nervous. I didn't want to appear weak to her.

"This isn't going to be easy, is it?" she asked, not beating around the bush.

"Nope," I replied. I gave in and looked out at the field all my childhood dreams had revolved around. My friends and former teammates were out there. Fans were already filling the stadium. The band was practicing. The drums could be heard all the way up here.

Tallulah moved and sat down, her feet dangling over the edge. "If my momma knew I was up here, she'd have a fit, possibly never recover. Cardiac arrest, even."

I took the waters from my pockets and handed her one, then sat down beside her. "Probably shouldn't tell her."

"If the cops take me in for breaking the law, she's gonna know. Then I'll be grounded until I'm thirty."

"That would suck but sounds a little dramatic."

She held out her hand. "You don't know my momma. Give me a burger. I'm starving."

I pulled out the burgers and left the fries in the bag to sit between us. "Might be cold since it took so long to get you up here."

She smirked. "This is the first time I've been asked to do something illegal."

That made me forget about the football field and my not being on it. The drums in the background faded, and I threw my head back and laughed. The weight on my chest eased. I didn't care about what I was missing. I had this. And this was turning out to be better.

"What's so funny?" she asked, then took a big bite of her burger.

"You. We aren't smuggling cocaine, or breaking and entering. This is not that big of a deal. If we were caught, they'd give us a slap on the wrist and a lecture on safety."

She swallowed her food, then shrugged. "Probably. But it's more exciting to think we're rebels breaking the law."

"Is it, now?" I replied.

She nodded and took another bite. Tallulah wasn't like any other girl I had dated. She wasn't flirting or trying to control me with the promise of sex. She was . . . real. Fun. And damned if I didn't regret all the years I had missed out not getting to know her.

Didn't Figure You Wanted My
Opinion on Your Love Life

CHAPTER 19

TALLULAH

I wasn't scared of heights. Not normal heights. So I hadn't been lying to Nash when he had asked. I thought of heights like climbing into the attic, or the tree house I always wanted as a kid but my mother was too scared to build for me. I didn't think Nash had been asking if I was scared of climbing a sixty-foot water tower.

When he had driven up here and I realized I was meant to climb this thing . . . I'd considered backing out, telling him no way. But the look of excitement in his eyes as he waited on my response kept me from doing that. I figured it was a slim chance I'd fall to my death. I'd more likely die in a car accident than fall off this water tower.

Now that we were up here looking out at the town we both called home, I was glad I hadn't let fear stop me. I hadn't really been concerned we would get arrested. I knew the cops were all waiting on the game to start. Doing their due diligence to make it safe as the opposing team arrived and the roads began to fill up leading into the parking lot. The police had simply been my excuse.

"Are you still planning on standing on the sidelines tonight?" I asked him after we finished our dinner.

He nodded. "Yeah. I am."

His gaze was out on that field as his friends warmed up and the band played in the stands. Although we couldn't hear them, we both knew they were pumped up and calling out whatever football players yell at one another before a game to prepare themselves mentally. The grass would be freshly cut, and the smell of grilled meat would fill the air as the concession stand got ready to feed the fans. My heart ached for him. I'd never loved anything like that. Never had something be that important to me. It had to be a void in his life.

"What happened? To your leg?" I asked before I could think that through and stop myself.

He sighed and turned his gaze to me. "A stupid backyard game of football. We do it every year on Memorial Day. Most folks just play flag or touch when not wearing pads. But we like to tackle. Makes it more fun." He looked pained as he said it. "Never thought once that it could change everything. I thought I was invincible. The harder the hit I took or gave the better. I was tough. I was an idiot."

He closed his eyes briefly and shook his head. The memory was hard on him. I wished I hadn't asked. If I could have taken back my question, I would have. Go back to the witty banter and laughter from earlier. That's what he needed right now, not being reminded of all he'd lost.

"I couldn't move my leg. I'd never felt that kind of pain before. The world began to fade in and out from the severity of it. But I wouldn't let myself pass out. Not from pain. I had to stay awake. I needed to know what was wrong. I thought I'd broken something . . . I thought, 'Damn, I hope it's better before practice starts up.' But what I never considered was I'd have a torn ACL, torn MCL, and a pinned ankle. A fucking limp for the rest of my life."

I didn't know much about sports injuries, but I'd heard ACL tears were bad. Really bad. But he had more than that. Way more. "I'm so sorry." Seemed inadequate as I said it, but it came out of my mouth anyway. Because I *was* sorry. I wished he could go back and not play the game. I knew he wished it more than anyone.

"Me too. I figure I'll always be sorry," he replied.

There was a heaviness over us now. The easy happy

feeling from before completely gone. That was my fault. He'd needed to forget not recap. Especially before this game. I thought hard on anything else I could say to lighten the mood. Change the subject without seeming as if I didn't care.

"I shouldn't have asked. This wasn't what you needed to be thinking about."

The corner of his mouth lifted, and he turned his gaze back to me. "Blakely never asked. All she knew was I was hurt. I had to go to therapy, and I wouldn't be playing football anymore. She didn't even come to the hospital for my surgeries. She said hospitals made her nervous and smelled funny."

I didn't care for Blakely. I never had. She was self-absorbed. I had watched her when he had started dating her last year. I couldn't understand why he didn't see that she cared only for herself. He was a nice guy. They didn't fit.

"She didn't deserve you," I told him. "I knew that when you started dating her."

He shifted his body until he was facing me completely. "You should have told me. Saved me the trouble." He was teasing now. His tone lighter. His eyes no longer held the shadows of his loss.

"Didn't figure you wanted my opinion on your love life."

He laughed then. "Sex life, Tallulah. There was no love there. Unless you count the love Blakely has for herself."

My cheeks burned at the word *sex*. Which was silly. We were seventeen. I was quite possibly the only girl in my grade who hadn't had sex. I hadn't even kissed a guy. Not even a peck. I needed to watch my HBO. Get over my awkwardness with the word *sex*.

"Why are you blushing?" he asked with a full grin now on his handsome face.

I shrugged. I tried to think of a believable lie and decided against it. The truth was better. Besides, it wasn't like the truth would shock him. He knew what I looked like last year. He also knew I hid in corners and had no social life.

"I am not used to talking about sex with . . . guys."

"So me saying 'sex life' made you blush?"

I nodded.

"Interesting. What if I say 'blow job'?"

His laughter got louder as my cheeks became an even brighter shade of red. I covered my face with my hands and tried desperately to make myself stop.

His laughter stopped. "I'm sorry," he said, still sounding amused. I had wanted to get his thoughts off his injury. I should be glad I'd achieved it. His hand touched my arm and gently tugged my left hand away from my face. "I shouldn't have laughed. It's cute. Fucking refreshing," he added.

I dropped my other hand and lifted my head back up. Turning to him, I smiled. "It's embarrassing."

He shook his head. "No, it's not." His voice had dropped and sounded more serious. I stared at his eyes, trying to figure out why when he began to move closer to me. His head lowering, his body easing my way until there was no space between us. I knew it was coming. Even though it had never happened to me before. I guess it was instinct. You just knew.

When his mouth touched mine, I forgot to breathe. It was the most exotic feeling in the world. The softness of his lips brushing over mine. His breath warm against my face. Even his heartbeat was fast against my chest. Or was that mine? I wasn't sure. All I knew was this was my first kiss, and I couldn't imagine anything ever being this perfect.

She'd Been Right There All Along
CHAPTER 20

NASH

The kiss was different. I didn't know how exactly. It had shaken me, made me question every kiss before and then regret them. I wished this had been my first. The others hadn't meant something. This had.

It was Tallulah's first. Her trembling hands as they rested on my arms and the way she inhaled sharply when my lips had first touched hers. The gentle way she tested it. Was unsure yet curious. All that should have made the kiss awkward. Instead it had made it the best I'd ever had.

I didn't want to leave this water tower. Stay up here with her in my arms. Being alone and forgetting what waited for me below was tempting. Up here she was mine. She made me laugh. Made me want other things. She made me want to find a new dream. Losing the field wasn't as important to me as it had been. Tallulah's tender, inexperienced kiss held more power than she would ever realize.

After I had pulled back from the kiss and looked into her eyes so honest and sincere, she'd laid her head on my chest and sighed. A content sound. My arms were still wrapped around her, and my gaze wasn't on that field down there. It was on Tallulah. The way she fit against me. It was as if she was what I had been waiting for. And she'd been right there all along.

"It's time for you to get down there," she said softly as she lifted her head to gaze up at me.

"Probably," I agreed, not loosening my grip. "I'd rather we stay right here."

She smiled then. A shy smile that made my heart squeeze. "I'd like that too. But they're expecting you. I think you'll regret it if you don't do this."

She was right. They all wanted me there like I always had been. Especially Ryker. I could be selfish and say they didn't get it. How hard it was going to be and what they expected of me. But I knew that reaction would let Tallulah down. I would eventually let her down. I just didn't want it to be tonight. This soon.

"I guess I better do this, then," I said, wishing I could kiss her again and we could forget it all.

Her hand rested on my heart. "You'll be glad you did."

I wish I had her optimism in life. To see everything in the light she did. Unfortunately, I didn't. Not anymore. I'd been handed heartbreak. I knew what it felt like. I hoped she never would.

The climb back down the tower wasn't nearly as exciting. The darkness was now thick enough that if I had glanced up, I wouldn't have seen up her short skirt. Not really. Maybe some shadows. I kept my focus on getting us down safely.

At the bottom she slipped her boots back on and then gave me a bright hopeful grin. "I'll never forget this first date."

Me either.

"That was the plan. I needed to blow Asa's measly field party date out of the water. Thought long and hard on how to do that." Only part of that was an exaggeration.

I didn't actually think his date would be hard to top. That night had sucked for everyone.

I slipped my hand over hers, and she threaded her fingers through mine. Our walk to the Escalade was quiet. My head was still up on the water tower with her in my arms. If I was lucky, so was hers. Words didn't seem needed at the moment. We were good like this. Comfortable in each other's presence.

I opened the passenger-side door and helped her as she climbed inside. I wanted to lean in and kiss her again, but that first kiss . . . it seemed too special to mess with just yet. Keeping it singular and on a pedestal for a little longer felt right. Instead I squeezed her hand and held her gaze longer than necessary before closing the door and going to get in the driver's seat.

"Who will you sit with at the game?" I asked her, not having thought about that before. "You could sit with my folks. I could introduce you to my mother."

"That's okay. I didn't plan on sitting with anyone. I was just going to find an empty seat. Tonight will be hard on your parents, too, I imagine. They don't need a stranger there beside them whom they feel they have to talk to."

My mother would be more than happy to meet Tallulah. She'd talk her damn head off. Possibly pull up my baby pictures on her Facebook and start showing her. Might not be the best idea after all. Tallulah was sweet, but my mother could scare her off. "If you're sure. My mom won't mind, though. She's nosy as fuck. Chatty too."

Her soft giggle felt good. Made it easier to deal with driving into the parking lot of a football game with the fans. I'd never done this before. I was always on that field before the fans arrived. Even as a kid, I was the water boy and the ball boy. The sidelines were all I knew.

"It's packed," she said, looking around. She was also changing the subject. I wouldn't push her to sit with my parents. I didn't like the idea of her sitting alone, but it was clear she was used to it. Seemed to prefer it.

"Yeah. First game is always a big one. If we win, it'll get bigger next week." The word *we* stuck in my throat. It wasn't a we. It was a they.

She didn't say anything more while I found a parking spot and turned off the engine. Staring straight ahead, I saw people walking with their stadium cushions, shakers, and even some cowbells. Football was life here in Alabama. Always had been.

"I'll sit to the far left toward the top. If you need to . . . look away. Or just take a moment. Find me. I'll be there."

I hadn't ever looked up into the crowd while on that field. My head had been on the game only. Nothing else. But tonight, knowing I had her to look back at—it helped. "Thanks. I'll find you before it starts. So I know where I'm looking."

She reached for her door, and I opened mine quickly. "No, wait," I told her, climbing down and jogging around the front of my SUV to get her door for her. "My momma would beat my ass if I let a woman open a door."

"And my momma would say, 'Tallulah, don't ever depend on a man for anything. You can do it all. If you want one, fine. But don't ever need one.'"

My chest rumbled with laughter. I liked that. If I had a daughter, I would tell her the same thing. "My momma needs to get to know yours. They'd like each other."

Tallulah stepped out and looked at the field. "Time to stop procrastinating. Go on. They're expecting you at the field house."

"I was going to walk you to the gate first," I told her.

She shook her head. "You see that line up there? It will take too long. I'm a big girl. I got this. Now go be part of your team."

I started to say something but decided that we'd had enough time to soak in that first kiss. Because right now I needed the second one. Closing the distance between us, I slid a hand around her waist and tugged her close before placing my mouth firmly on hers. Just enough pressure to taste her. When she opened to me, my knees felt weak, and I let my enjoyment go on a little longer. This could get me through anything.

It was her that pulled back this time. Then, with a gentle shove, she whispered, "Go on."

I did. Glancing back just once before I headed to join the others. I was late. They'd complain, but what could

they really do? It wasn't like I was playing. I was just there
for support. As if they needed more.

Just before I got down the hill that led to the field house,
I smelled the distinct scent of weed. Pausing, I surveyed the
area, and the tiny orange burn on the paper caught my attention. Stepping out of the darkness was a guy who looked
somewhat familiar. But I couldn't place him. He didn't live
around here. That much was obvious. His pale blond hair
brushed his shoulders, and the tight jeans he was wearing,
along with the shirt that had holes in it but you could tell it
was purchased like that, screamed out-of-towner.

He smirked at me. Took one last drag, then dropped
it to the gravel before stepping on it and walking off. The
dude was going to just leave pot right there. Was he serious?

"What the fuck?" I said, and he paused. Gave me one
more look.

"Problem?" he asked with amusement in his tone.

"This is Alabama, man. Pot's not fucking legal." Not
that I wasn't guilty of smoking some a time or two.

The guy nodded. "Don't have to remind me where I
am. This is my hell now," he said, holding out both his
arms and backing away.

I was late. I had no time to argue with him about tossing weed down on the ground. "Whatever," I muttered,
and left him there.

God, Could This Place
Be Any More Cliché?

CHAPTER 21

TALLULAH

Throughout the first half Nash looked up at me four times. That's all I had seen. Him. I'd watched him the entire time. Studied his stance, how he interacted with the others, and hoped this wasn't as difficult as it appeared it was.

Not to anyone else. He was slapping guys on the back. Talking to them about plays and cheering them on. It was when he had to look back at me that I knew this was killing him. His needing my reassurance and support said more than any acting job he did on that field.

The team had gone into the field house, and the fans were up talking, getting snacks, and I was alone. No one really knew me. I was used to this. Being without a group of friends. What I wasn't used to was people noticing me. I felt eyes on me. I was no longer ignored. Needing to get away from the crowd and all the chattering, I went to find a quieter spot. Take a breather and not feel as if I stood out, sitting there with no one around me. No one to talk to.

When you reached the bottom of the stands, to your right was the concession stand and restrooms. The herd was headed that way. Filling in every available patch of grass. I went left. Fewer people, more room to move. I kept going until the back gate that led to the overflow parking lot was in my view. No one was there. I walked over to the gate to wait for the crowd to move on and there was no one around. It was darker back here, and there was no view of the field. Not a popular place to be unless it was two teenagers making out.

"This place is whacked, and you sitting up there all alone is just fucking sad. What did you do? Kill the town's favorite pup?"

The masculine voice startled me. It wasn't familiar nor was it from around here. There was no accent. At all. Nothing. Weird. And possibly unsafe. I spun around to see a guy leaning against the fence farther in the shadows. He was alone. From what I could make out, he had longish hair, and it was such a light color it reflected the moonlight.

I didn't know him. And I'd seen enough *CSI* to know

this wasn't the best idea, to stand out here alone with this stranger. I began moving away.

He laughed. It was a rich, amused laugh. "God, could this place be any more cliché?"

I paused.

"Football on Friday nights, fucking cowboy boots on with a blue-jean skirt, lettermen jackets on girls' shoulders, and it's still eighty goddamn degrees out here. Oh, and the cowbells. Can't forget the cowbells. Those are priceless." He ended his rant and pulled out a lighter. When the small flame lit, he held a cigarette to his lips. "Don't call for the cops, Daisy May. It's just regular ole nicotine."

I should have gone, forgotten this completely. But he shifted, and the light that was peeping over the stands from the lights on the field illuminated and I saw him clearer. He didn't seem dangerous. He was tall, slender; something caught the light on both his ears, and I saw that his white-blond hair was much longer than I had thought. It was tucked behind his ears. The clothes he was wearing stood out the most. He wasn't dressed like a guy from Lawton. He reminded me of someone from *90210*. And he was calling us cliché?

"Which one of those meatheads do you belong to? Gotta be one of them. You can't take your eyes off that field. I'd have noticed you anyway because you're a stunner, but you know that already. I've seen a lot of beautiful women. Not like you're unique. But I do notice when people behave out of the norm. You've got on your Daisy May costume, but you aren't acting like the others. You don't care that you are alone, nor do you check to see if people are watching you. Hell, I watched you for over an hour, and you never looked my way. Fascinating as fuck."

I didn't like this guy. Walking off was the best idea. But he was right. I was alone, and I would have to go right back up there while they all talked excitedly about the two-touchdown lead we had and stuffed their faces with nachos.

"Who are you?" I asked instead.

He chuckled, took a couple more steps into the light. I could see him clearly now. His bright green eyes were unnatural and had to be contacts. If not, he was an alien, or possibly a vampire, and I'd just stepped into one of my paranormal books I loved so much. My bet was it was simply contacts. "Do you still need an answer, or do you know?" he asked.

How the heck would I know who he was just because he was standing in the light? "We've never met. I'd remember your fake eye color and diamond-studded earrings," I replied in a more annoyed tone than I meant to.

He ran a hand over his face and muffled more amusement. "This place really is antiquated. Tell me—do you all have smartphones, or is it still flip phones? Or better yet, landlines?"

I had never had a more confusing conversation in my life. He was jumping from one subject to the next. Halftime was about to end, and I needed to get to my seat. This was a waste of time.

I turned and started to walk away.

"The one with the limp, that one's yours," he called out.

I wasn't convinced this guy was safe. He was a bit creepy with his knowledge. Stalker like.

"He's the only one on that field who wishes he was somewhere else."

I agreed. But then I had been studying Nash all night. Paying attention to his body language. Worrying about him. I glared back at the guy one more time. "Who are you!" I demanded.

He tilted his head and ran his hand through his long hair like some model in a commercial. It was odd and annoying all at once. He really liked himself. He was the male version of Blakely. Except I would guess he was smarter. This conversation had been the weirdest one in my life to date, but he hadn't spoken like an empty-headed ditz. I was beginning to worry he was a serial killer, with his deep observations and interest in people he didn't know.

"You ever watched YouTube? Or do the folks down

here know what the Internet is?" The way he asked the last part was with a very bad imitation drawl. Like he was making fun of the way we talked.

"You've got to be the rudest person I have ever spoken to," I replied. "Of course we have smartphones, we use personal laptops in the classroom, our textbooks are all online, and although I don't watch YouTube, I do know what it is. My mother watches cooking tutorials on it all the time." After I said all that I wished I could take it back. I should have walked away. This guy was not stable. He was sketchy. And I needed to shut up and go on.

The scoreboard buzzed, ending halftime.

"I have to go," I said before moving away from him, and quickly. He didn't call out anything else. I made it to the stairs and headed up to my seat, not once glancing back to see if he was following me. When I reached my seat and sat down, I was suddenly thankful to be surrounded by all the people. It was comforting. I found Nash, and he turned to look up at me just as I spotted him. He smiled. I let out a sigh of relief that I was here and back where I was supposed to be. He gave me a small salute and went back to talking to Ryker, who was in full pads standing beside him.

For the first time all night I took in my surroundings. I saw the groups of people and noticed the cowbells being shaken loudly from the stands. Blue shakers covered the place, and cheers for the Lions rang in the air. I started to return my gaze to Nash when my eyes locked on the guy. He was at the bottom, in the farthest left corner. He wasn't sitting, and no one seemed to notice him. His focus was on me. When he saw me looking back, he smirked and nodded his head toward the field in Nash's direction, then ducked out. He was gone, and I was more than glad to see him go.

Nice to See How the Other Half Lived
CHAPTER 22

NASH

The smell of the bonfire was a Friday night norm. What I knew. Coming here had been the last thing I wanted to do, but I needed a beer. I also didn't want to chance Tallulah trying to talk to me about tonight. About the game. How it felt. That kind of thing. I was moody. I wanted to be alone.

Asking Tallulah out for after the game had been me hoping that would get my mind off things. The mood the game would put me in hadn't been something I had considered. Here we were now. Ryker talking about the one play of the game he scored. It had been impressive. And he wanted to recap it. Over and over.

That had been me last year and the year before. It

annoyed me now, but I drank my beer and kept my mouth shut. Tallulah didn't seem relaxed or like she was enjoying this. I didn't blame her. I wasn't much fun. If I wanted another date with her, I needed to try harder. Stop being a damn baby about the game.

They'd won by three touchdowns. It had been a fairly easy win. If I wasn't so fucking self-absorbed with my pity party, I'd be happy for them. I was trying to be, but it wasn't coming through. I slipped an arm around Tallulah's waist and tugged her closer to me. "Sorry this is boring," I whispered.

She turned her head and tilted it back slightly to look up at me. Up close she was flawless. I hadn't thought about that earlier. I'd been too busy with that kiss. Now I could appreciate it.

"I'm not bored. Just taking it all in. This is what y'all have been up to for the past three years on Friday nights while I sat in my room with a book. Nice to see how the other half lived." The smile curving her lips was teasing.

"I'm sure with all this excitement you regret missing every moment of it," I replied.

She sighed dramatically. "Well of course I do. One cannot get enough of Ryker replaying his best moment on the field fifty different ways, or Blakely doing everything but stripping to keep Hunter's attention on her alone. The best are the cheerleaders, who still think they need to do routines after they've drunk a few too many."

I laughed loudly. She was right. Completely. Her description could not have been more accurate. "I can assume you will be on board with attending all these with me this year, then?" There was no way I was coming to these every Friday night. It didn't hold the same appeal as it once had. I no longer fit. But I was sure she knew that.

She pressed a finger to her chin as if in deep thought. Then gave me a serious expression meant to be mocking. "Only if Asa and Ryker will talk incessantly about themselves and the cheerleaders will be a little more annoying. Then possibly I will return."

I squeezed her waist. "I'd say I will see what I can do, but I am pretty sure those are all a given." I nodded my head toward the trees, where all the cars were parked behind. "Let's go."

She smiled. "Good."

I turned back to the group that hadn't even realized we'd been in our own private conversation. "We're out. Y'all party on," I called.

They didn't ask me why I was going. But I could see surprise in their eyes. I normally shut these parties down.

I waved as they called out good-byes, but I didn't stay around long enough for them to ask me to stay. Or where we were headed. Tallulah responded to those who told her they were glad she had come. Although these people had ignored her in the past, she was polite. Didn't seem to hold bitterness toward them.

"I swear he was there," a girl with a loud high-pitched voice said from the group we were passing.

"You're insane. There is no way that Haegan Baylor was in Lawton, Alabama, at a football game. You need to stop watching him so much. You're starting to hallucinate," Blakely said.

"I know Haegan Baylor. I would know the back of his head if that is all I saw. I've seen every YouTube video he has ever done. He posts a new vlog three times a week. And he said he was moving in his last vlog. He was here!" The other girl I now recognized as Pamela was loudly defending her belief.

"Sorry, Pam. I don't believe that. No one else saw him," Blakely replied.

We kept walking, but I noticed Tallulah's attention was drawn to their conversation. "You know who this Haegan Baylor is?" I asked her. She didn't seem like one who would watch vloggers. I'd never watched one, but Blakely watched a couple weekly like it was part of her life. Then she talked about them constantly, as if I cared.

Tallulah looked away from them, then shook her head. "No, I'm not sure what a vlog is."

That was shocking. But then this was Tallulah. She was different. Which I loved.

"There are these people who do these videos, kind of like a reality television show, and then post them on YouTube. Some are better at it than others. Many have gotten famous from it. They call themselves vloggers. But from what I've seen, it's mostly teens videoing boring shit they do and doing stupid stuff to get more viewers."

Tallulah frowned. "They get famous? Seriously?"

"Yep. Blakely was stressing out over getting some backpack for school back in June that one of those vloggers she likes was selling in his merch store."

"His what?" she asked incredulously.

"They sell merchandise in online stores. The popular ones do." I thought it was crazy too, but Blakely was worried it would sell out and was on her computer at the time it was released to be sure to get it. I'd forgotten about that until now.

We reached my truck, and Tallulah paused at the door. "I think . . ." Then she shook her head. "Never mind."

I opened her door, and she climbed inside. I wanted to know what she was going to say, but I didn't push her. I still needed to come up with somewhere for us to go. I didn't want to take her home just yet.

When I was inside, I saw her yawn and cover it up with

her hand. I wasn't ready to give her up, but I knew she was tired. "You're sleepy," I said to her.

If she argued, I was going to keep her longer.

"Yeah, a little," she agreed.

Damn.

"Okay then, we can call it a night." I paused. "What are you doing tomorrow?" That may have sounded a little too needy. But it came out before I could think it through.

She ducked her head, and I could see the smile on her face. She liked that I had asked. I felt better about it. "I help Mom clean the house on Saturday mornings. We're normally finished around one in the afternoon. Then, nothing really."

Fuck being cool. I wasn't cool anymore anyway. "There's a trail I like to hike. Goes to a cold spring that's pretty this time of year. I think you'd like it." I hadn't dated a girl I thought would enjoy this. I always hiked it alone.

"Sounds nice. I'm sure I would."

"Would you be ready by three?" I asked.

She nodded. "Yeah. Three is good."

And just like that my first Friday night not spent in pads and playing the sport I loved turned into something better.

Something about a Unicorn Wall
CHAPTER 23

TALLULAH

The tenderness when I first opened my eyes and swallowed made me pause. That was not good. Today I could not get sick. I threw my covers off and went downstairs, trying to ignore the slow-building headache. My stomach turned as I opened the fridge, and I had to stop and lean against the counter a moment. I was suddenly weak.

Closing my eyes, I inhaled deeply. Tried to will all these symptoms away. Then opened my eyes and stood straighter with a fight that died the moment the kitchen began to spin. I had to grab the counter again. I definitely felt off.

"Good morning. Are you going to start in the kitchen today . . . honey?" Mom was instantly beside me, although I couldn't see her because I was having to keep my eyes closed from the spinning. My stomach wasn't handling it well, and my head was now hurting so bad I winced with each pound.

"You're burning up. Come to the sofa." Mom's arm was around me, and I let her lead me to the living room, which was closer than my bedroom. I sank down onto the sofa and curled my knees up under my chin. I heard a whimper. I thought it was me.

The pain in my head was battling with the now raw throat I had, not to mention every time I tried to open my eyes, the spinning was there. I had to be still, pray that it ended soon.

"Sit up." Mom was beside me, pulling me into her arms. "You have to take this to get your fever down. You also need to drink some liquids. When did this start?"

Too many words. I managed to open my mouth and swallow the pill, although it was painful. The cold water felt good to my throat, but it still hurt when I swallowed.

"Have you been like this all night?"

I shook my head and lay back down. A cold cloth was placed on my forehead. And my body began to tremble from chills. My mom had a blanket over me before the first shiver ended. "Can you tell me what hurts?" she asked.

I loved her, but I needed her to stop asking me things. Talking was too much.

"All of it," I whispered, and shivered again.

"Okay, I'll wait, but if this doesn't bring your fever down and help enough in a few hours, we are going to the doctor."

I wasn't sure how we would do that when I couldn't get off the sofa. The world slowly faded, along with my mother's talking.

The next time I heard anything, it was the vacuum cleaner coming from the hallway. I opened my eyes and waited for the pounding headache. It was duller now. My throat still hurt terribly. I reached for the cup of water beside me, and the ice had melted. I took a drink, hoping it would help. It didn't.

I started to move, and my entire body felt too weak. I sank back down and closed my eyes. The pounding was returning, and my body was aching now. Closing my eyes, I gave in to the darkness and faded out again.

My mother's voice telling someone I had woken up very ill and hadn't been able to do more than sleep all day was what I heard when I woke again. I almost closed my eyes and ignored it when I remembered Nash. We had a date today. I had forgotten. I tried to move and sit up when I heard Mom say something else. Then the door closed. I couldn't get all the way up. I gave up and sighed in frustration.

Mom walked into the room, and I stared up at her. I wanted to ask, but it hurt to talk.

"That was Nash. He was here to pick you up. I told him you were sick. He said to tell you he hoped you felt better soon. How do you feel?" she asked as she knelt in front of me and put her hand on my forehead. "Your fever was down, but you're hot again. I'm getting you another aspirin—then we're going to the after-hours clinic. This could be the flu."

"I can't get up," I moaned, closing my eyes. The idea of going to the bathroom was difficult, much less walking out to the car and going to the doctor.

"We could end up in the emergency room tonight if I don't take you now."

She wasn't kidding. If I didn't get better, she'd haul me to the ER in the middle of the night. The idea of sitting around all night feeling like this in a waiting room gave me the strength to sit up. "Can you bring me a bra? I am wearing this," I said in a hoarse whisper. Anything more was too painful.

"Sure. Stay right there. Try and drink more. I got you some fresh water."

I nodded and took a sip as she hurried out of the room. The Gryffindor tank top and cut-off sweatpants I had slept in would have to do for this outing. I didn't normally go places with shorts this short, but right now I just didn't care.

Mom came back with my bra and helped me get it on. "Do you want me to brush your hair?" she asked.

"I don't care," I replied. I wanted to lie here in my misery.

She ran her hand over it. "It's fine. Let's go."

I let her help me up because I couldn't do anything myself. The walk to the car felt like the longest distance in my life. I had to stop several times and lean on her. She patted my head and reassured me it wasn't much farther.

Once we finally made it to the car, I collapsed in the passenger seat and moaned. Mom laid my seat back, and I curled back up into the fetal position and prayed I didn't die before we got there. I wasn't positive this was the best idea. All my symptoms were in full-on attack now that I had moved.

Mom cranked the car, and the AC was cold. It cooled my forehead and made me shiver at the same time.

"They can give you a shot, hopefully, that will help fast," Mom said, trying to make me feel better about this. "Staying home isn't going to get you better. You've got to be checked out, honey."

I couldn't even nod my head to let her know I understood. All my energy was gone from the walk out here.

"Last night must have gone good since you had a date again today with Nash. When you're better, I look forward to hearing all about it. I'm sure he had a tough night not getting to play. I'm glad you went."

I fell asleep while Mom chatted on about Nash, football, and dates. I think at one point she was talking about brownies, but I wasn't sure. I couldn't stay awake, and her talking was exhausting. Just before I was completely gone, I heard her say something about a unicorn wall. I had no idea what she was talking about. I had missed part of that conversation.

When the car stopped, I opened my eyes and knew there was no way I was going to be able to stand up. I closed my eyes again and hoped she would just leave me in here.

Was This Part of His Vlog Shit?
CHAPTER 24

NASH

There were places I could be. Things I could do. But I wasn't in the mood for my friends. Instead, I sat on a wooden picnic table in the park away from the screaming kids and their mothers and stared out at the town while I drank the soda I'd gotten from the Stop and Go across the street.

I'd woken up looking forward to spending the day with Tallulah. But she was sick. Her mother actually looked worried and stressed out as she told me about it, so I believed her. Tallulah hadn't been trying to get out of our date, which was good. Sucked that she was sick, though.

"What's the story with your leg?" a male voice asked me, and I shifted my eyes from the center-of-town caution light to the guy who had quietly walked up on me, or I'd just been so lost in my thoughts I hadn't noticed. The blond hair was the only reason I recognized him from last night. He'd been the crazy-ass pot smoker I'd passed on my way to the field house.

"Excuse me?" I was annoyed. This guy was rude.

He looked unconcerned by my glare and pointed to my leg. "The leg, your limp—you stood on the sidelines all night. What's the story?"

Was he for fucking real? "Who the hell are you?" I asked him instead.

He smirked and shook his head. "I've only spoken to two people in this town, and neither of you know who I am. I thought I was going to hate it here. I still may. But this being anonymous thing is nice. I'd forgotten what that was like."

This was one cocky bastard. "Why would we know who you are? You're not from around here. That's for damn sure."

He gave one single nod. "I'm one of the lucky ones. Not born in Mayberry hell."

He was a douche. I looked back at the traffic light and took a drink of my soda. Maybe if I ignored him he'd go away.

"Not going to tell me about that leg? Fine. I'll ask your girl."

That got my attention. "What?"

He seemed pleased with my reaction. "The hot loner blonde who watched you all night. We spoke. I don't think she cares for me either. You southern folks are supposed to be all nice and friendly. I'm not finding that so here. The West Coast has gotten a bad rap. We're fucking friendly compared to this bunch."

He'd talked to Tallulah. She hadn't said anything.

"What do you want?" I asked him, not in the mood to defend southern hospitality.

He leaned against the tree beside him. "You've got a story. Possibly the only interesting thing other than your girl that I have seen in this town. I like stories. It's my thing. Human interest. Entertainment. That kind of shit."

The word *entertainment* was what brought last night's overheard conversation back to me. I'd forgotten, since it hadn't been important. I hadn't cared. But it was all clicking into place now. Pam hadn't been wrong after all.

"You're the YouTube vlogger guy." As I said it, a slow smile spread across his face.

"Surprising. I wouldn't have guessed you watched vlogs."

"I don't. But girls in this town do. You were spotted last night."

He sighed and nodded. "Probably shouldn't have gone

to the game. But then Monday they'll see me. Can't hide at motherfucking school."

School? He was going to go to our school? Here in Lawton? "Let me get this straight," I said, finally interested in something this guy had to say. "You are some famous YouTube guy from LA, and you're in Lawton, Alabama, to go to school?" None of that made sense. These guys got sponsors and shit. They were supposed to be loaded. Why would he be moving from LA to Alabama? Was this part of his vlog shit?

"When your mother catches your father fucking your little brother's college-age nanny in the pool, then shit happens. It was stay with the dick that is my father in LA, or go with my mother to the town she grew up in so she could be near her parents to deal with life. I couldn't let Lil Jo leave town without me. Mom is a big girl, and she can handle it. Lil Jo is only five. He needs me. So here the fuck I am," he finished with his hands held out. "Now what's your story? You got mine."

He was here because of his family. Did he even realize how hard it was going to be on him once the rest of Lawton found out? He wasn't going to have a normal life here. They wouldn't let him. This was not LA. Celebrities weren't walking the streets daily.

"They'll never leave you alone. You won't be able to go

anywhere without drawing attention," I told him.

He shrugged. "Maybe. Will make for some good vlog action in the beginning I guess. I figure it'll wear off."

Seeing as I had never watched a vlog, I wasn't sure what he videoed exactly. "How's that work? Your vlog shit. What is it you video?"

He shifted and pulled something out of his pocket, then tossed it in the air and caught it as if it were a ball. "This is one of the many cameras I use." It was small. Like a little box almost. He then reached into his back pocket and pulled out something else that, when he unfolded it, was a stick. "This is a stabilizer," he explained. Then he attached the camera to the stick and held it out.

"No school yet. Still trying to figure this place out. There is seriously nothing here. I take back what I said about hell. There's got to be more action there. Not fair to compare the two." He was talking to the camera. Then it was directed at me. "This guy won't tell me shit. It's the one from last night on the sidelines. He's got a story. Just haven't figured it out yet."

I glared up at the small, offending camera. "Get that thing off me," I grumbled.

"He's got a stellar personality, too."

"He doesn't want the damn camera in his face," I said instead.

"Just tell us why you limp. I told you about my dad banging the nanny. The least you could do is tell me why you limp."

Was that camera on? "Are you recording this? You just said the shit about your dad," I pointed out. I knew he had millions of viewers.

He chuckled. "Hell yeah, I'm recording it. They know. I already explained why I was leaving LA. Watch my damn vlog. This shit gets edited. What we're doing now would be boring as hell without some edits. But every time I can tell the world about my douchebag dad, I will."

I shook my head. "You're seriously fucked up."

"You've not seen anything," he told me. "Come with me. I'll show you fucked up."

If I sat and thought about it too long, I'd say no. I didn't really like this guy. But I didn't think about it. Instead, I stood up. "Okay. Show me."

I'm Still Not Convinced It Was Legal

CHAPTER 25

TALLULAH

The flu lasted three more days. I was weak and out of it. Nash texted a few times, checking on me, and I replied, but it hadn't been anything too detailed. Today, however, I was better. I took a shower and ate some toast and fruit. I felt like living again.

I dreaded the schoolwork I had missed. I would spend the rest of the week trying to catch up. I had almost texted Nash to tell him I was coming back to school this morning but then wasn't sure if I should. Would he care? Our connection seemed so distant now. Not having seen or talked to him since Friday night, I felt weird. Unsure.

Walking into school, I saw a buzz in the hallway, and

girls were more silly than normal. When I caught a glimpse of the guy from the football game Friday night, it came back to me. I'd forgotten. He must have been the YouTube guy after all. Why was he here? In Lawton of all places.

"You're back," Nash said, coming up beside me.

I was suddenly nervous. "Yeah, I started feeling more like me last night."

"Good." He grinned. He seemed happy. The moody guy from last week at school was gone. This was the Nash I remembered. "I missed you."

I was missed. I couldn't remember one time that I had missed school over the years when someone had told me they missed me. "Really?" I asked, then felt my cheeks heat at the pathetic way that simple question sounded.

"Tallulah, glad you're back. Wasn't the same in class without you." Mr. Dace was smiling as he stopped in front of us. His gaze was on me, though. He wasn't focused on Nash at all.

"Thanks. I had the flu," I explained quickly.

His eyes looked concerned. "That sucks. You take your time with the makeup work. Don't overwork yourself."

I nodded, thinking there was no way I was going to take my time.

He finally cut his eyes toward Nash, then nodded once—"Nash"—before he walked on down the hallway.

"I really hate that guy," Nash muttered.

"Mr. Dace?" I asked, surprised. I didn't think anyone could hate Mr. Dace. I knew he hadn't wanted to be at that field party anyway the night Mr. Dace had broken it up. There was no reason for him to hate Mr. Dace.

He lifted both his eyebrows as if that was an understood thing. I was going to ask him why when someone else joined us.

"Looks like the girlfriend is back from the dead," the guy from the football game said as he came up beside Nash and put his arm around his shoulders as if they were friends. Nash didn't shrug him off or look surprised.

"Tallulah, this is Haegan. Haegan, this is Tallulah. I know the two of you have spoken before, but here's your official introduction."

I frowned and looked from Haegan to Nash. "You know him?" I asked, confused.

"Missed a lot those days you were down sick," Haegan said.

Nash looked apologetic. "Turns out Haegan was the YouTuber that Pam saw that night. She hadn't been wrong."

Haegan Baylor the vlogger? Really?

"Walk me to class, Haegan," Blakely said, not even caring that Haegan was standing with Nash.

Haegan rolled his eyes and appeared to ignore her.

"He promised to walk *me*. Didn't you, Haegan?" another cheerleader said, pushing closer.

"No he didn't. He hasn't said he'd walk anyone," Pam announced with authority, like she was his stage manager.

Other girls began to crowd around us, and I started to feel claustrophobic. I needed out of this herd of crazy. My eyes met Nash's, and he shrugged like this was normal. Had he been dealing with this all week?

"I'll walk all of you. If you're going in that direction." Haegan pointed the opposite way from my classroom. Relief was instant.

When he started walking, the girls followed him like the insane clingy creeps they were. Nash and I were soon left alone again. He glanced toward the departing crowd then back at me. "He's not that bad. He deals with the fame well."

I hadn't said anything negative. I didn't know Haegan. It was the crowd he drew I hadn't been thrilled about. "How did you meet him?" I asked, realizing I had missed a lot this week.

"Saturday, when you got sick, I ended up at the park alone. Sitting off in the woods on a picnic table, staring at nothing. He showed up. Pushy as hell. Wouldn't go away. But you know"—he paused, then gave me a slow smile—"he's not bad. He's not football. He has a life that has nothing to do with all that. It's a good change for me."

That made sense. Haegan was a friend who wouldn't remind Nash of all he'd lost. "I'm glad you met him, then."

Nash gave me a small smirk. "I was on his latest vlog. It posts tonight. I didn't want to do it, but he insisted. Wasn't so bad. Was kind of fun. I'm still not convinced it was legal."

At the word *legal* I grew concerned, but Nash was smiling like it was the best thing ever, so I didn't say anything. Maybe he had been kidding. "I'll have to watch it," I said, hoping it wasn't going to get Nash in any trouble.

"Come to Haegan's with me tonight. He's posting it, and he wants me to come over and see what all he does when a vlog goes live. I wasn't sure you'd be back so I said yes. I'd rather spend time with you. If you don't want to go, we can do something else."

I didn't want to go to Haegan's. I still wasn't sold on this guy. He'd been so odd at the game. He'd tried to make me uncomfortable. I didn't like that. But Nash liked him, and I liked Nash. I had to give Haegan another chance.

"Okay. If Haegan doesn't mind," I replied, suddenly thinking Haegan might mind. He didn't seem like he'd want me around.

"He won't mind. I swear, he's the most laid-back person I have ever met."

The warning bell rang. Nash leaned over and pressed a

quick kiss to my lips. "Glad you're back," he whispered, surprising me. My cheeks heated, and my heart fluttered.

"Me too," I said with a shaky voice.

Nash saw my reaction, and his grin was a pleased one. "See you after class," he said, then turned and headed toward his next class.

I watched him go only a second before hurrying across the hall and three doors down to my first period. It wasn't until I was almost to my class that I realized . . . Nash's limp had been better. He'd walked straighter. Taller.

He was confident again.

I didn't know if it was me or Haegan who had inspired that. It didn't matter. He was changing. Back to the Nash I knew. The guy who smiled easy. The guy who walked like he had the world in his hands.

I Was Still Nash Fucking Lee
CHAPTER 26

NASH

The high-pitched scream caught my attention along with all the rest of the student body, and everyone began pouring into the hallway from their first-period class. The bell had just rung, and we'd all been moving slow as was typical for morning classes. Most of us needed caffeine. But you could bet a fight would wake us all up.

When I made it through the crowd, shoving to get a good view of what was more than likely two girls going at it from the scream we'd all heard, I saw Haegan with his hands up in the air, trying to stop whatever was going on. I pushed through and got close enough to see Pam, which was no surprise if this was about Haegan, and Julie Winters tied up. Pam had a handful of Julie's red curly hair, and Julie was slapping the shit out of Pam's face. It was already looking bright red.

The crowd was cheering and laughing. Haegan looked confused as hell and tried to no avail to calm them down. "Excuse me," I said to the guy in front of me. He stepped out of my way, and I almost got to Haegan before he made the mistake of stepping into that mix. Pam's elbow clocked him in the jaw, and she realized it with a horrified look.

The distraction, however, cost her a fist to the nose that wasn't that forceful, since Julie was five feet tall and about one hundred pounds on a good day. I was shocked she was in a fight. I couldn't remember ever seeing her fight before. Her temper was fierce for a tiny girl, but never like this.

Pam covered her nose as if that had actually hurt. "OHMYGOD!" she cried out. The damage she did to Haegan's jaw was no doubt worse than anything done to her nose. Julie shoved her in the chest. "Come on, bitch! You want to talk smack now!"

Pam's eyes went wide before clouding over into crazy as hell. Someone needed to get Julie out of her reach. Pam was taller and stronger.

"Jesus! What's wrong with the two of you?" Haegan said, grabbing Julie's arm this time and pulling her back. Bad idea.

Julie's brother wasn't tiny. Joseph Winters broke through the crowd at that time and knocked Pam into Haegan and then grabbed his sister to tuck her protectively against his side. "I don't care if you're a girl, Pam. Touch her again and I am beating your ass," Joseph warned her loudly.

"No one needs to hit the girls. They're mutually at fault here," Haegan said, stepping in front of Pam. I was impressed with that move. Had to give him credit. But Joseph was about to take this out on him, and I had to move fast. I shoved between the girls in front of me and stood beside Haegan to stare down Joseph. Didn't have any issue with the guy, but he needed to back off and take his sister with him. Haegan hadn't done anything.

"You challenging me, crip?" Joseph asked, taking a step toward me. That was the first time someone had actually called me a cripple. It didn't go over well. My hands clenched, and adrenaline surged through my body.

"What the fuck did you just say?" Ryker's voice carried loud, and people parted to let him through.

Joseph turned to see Ryker and Asa step up beside me.

"I asked if he was challenging me," Joseph said, his voice not so loud now. "I'm just getting my sister out of this crazy shit. I didn't come to fight."

Ryker stepped in front of me. Like I needed protecting. Like I was exactly what Joseph had just called me. Fuck that. I stepped around my cousin. "I don't need you to pro-tect me," I snarled. Pissed he thought that I did.

"Would you like me to show you exactly what this crip can do to you? Without their help," I said loud and clear for the onlookers to hear.

I could see in Joseph's eyes he wanted to take me up on it. But he wouldn't. Because he was afraid of the guys standing behind me. That stung. I needed to prove myself. I wanted them all to see that I was still me. I was still Nash Fucking Lee. Football didn't make me who I was. I could still whup his ass.

"I'm not fighting you," he said simply.

That was a trigger. I snapped. Just as I lunged at him, another female war cry went out, and arms wrapped around me, pulling me back. "Calm down or you're going to get suspended," Ryker said as he held me back. "Let Pam get in trouble instead."

I jerked free of his hold just as Pam slid back across the floor and Mandy B—I didn't know her last name—jumped on top of her, and they began pulling hair. What the fuck had happened now?

Haegan sighed in frustration and went to grab Mandy off Pam to stop this fight, but Mandy B's boyfriend grabbed Haegan's arm, and fists were thrown. I needed a fight. Ryker wasn't stopping this. I had something to prove. I swung, and my fist met Tim's right jaw. We'd played foot-ball together. We'd laughed together in the locker room. But none of that mattered. Not anymore.

"Stop it!" Coach D was suddenly in the middle of all this, and he was grabbing Haegan's arms and pulling him back. I hated the man. Seeing him there with his hands on my friend infuriated me. Where had he been when this shit started? Now he wanted to jump in and grab the wrong fucking person?

"Back the fuck off!" I all but roared as I started toward Coach D. "He's not the one you need to be grabbing!"

"Nash," Ryker's tone was warning.

"Excuse me? I don't believe I need confirmation from a violent teenage boy," Coach D replied, his cheeks red. He was angry. Good. Let him snap. His ass would get fired.

"You don't even know what's going on. Let him go!" I reached out to take Coach D's hands off Haegan myself.

Coach D released him. "Both of you to the principal's office."

Was he serious? There had been two girl brawls, and he was sending *us* to the office? What about Tim? "Just us? Out of all the fighting, you're sending us?" I asked incredu-lously. He had to be joking.

"I didn't see the others. I just saw you. And him. Now go."

The challenge in his eyes as he used the fucking authority he had was clear. He wanted me to fight this. He wanted me in trouble. He was a bigger dick than I realized.

"Nash, stop this. Just go." Tallulah's voice got my attention. Where did she come from?

When my eyes locked with hers, she looked upset. With me? Fuck, I'd done nothing wrong. "He knows I didn't start this. He's doing it because he doesn't like me. Notice none of the football players are going. Tim started this shit, and he's fucking free to go on to class."

Tallulah didn't seem to believe me. Her eyes said as much. She'd not seen this. She was just showing up.

"I'm not telling you again. Go to the office," Coach D said firmly.

"Come on, let's go," Haegan said, not looking too concerned about this.

"We didn't fucking do anything wrong," I argued.

"And he doesn't care," Haegan said, pointing out the obvious.

I glanced back at Tallulah. She was frowning. Disappointed. Fuck that. Whatever.

I started down the hallway, and Haegan fell into step beside me. "I got some of this shit on video. It's gonna make for a great vlog," he said once we were away from everyone else.

I turned to look at him and saw he was grinning.

"How the hell did you video that?"

He held out his wrist. It looked like some kind of watch. "This."

Well, damn.

CHAPTER 27

TALLULAH

I sat my books down on a desk. My stomach was in knots. Nash had been . . . different. Not as much like the old Nash either. Just different. He'd seemed angry at me, but I had been trying to get him to stop before he got suspended.

Haegan Baylor was not a good friend. I didn't know him really, but Nash had changed quickly in the short time he'd been around Haegan. Or at least it looked like it from what I had witnessed just now.

"Teenage boys have a lot of growing up to do. Don't look so down. It's typical. They're hotheaded, selfish, and it'll be years before they're smart enough to listen to a woman." Mr. Dace's voice startled me. The room had been

empty when I entered. Everyone was still out in the hallway talking about the fight, no doubt.

I shrugged, not wanting to look at Mr. Dace. I was close
to tears, and that seemed silly. I was embarrassed.

"Tallulah, don't let it upset you. He'll regret it once he
figures out he was an ass."

Had he been an ass? Or was I overreacting? I lifted my
head and met Mr. Dace's concerned gaze. "He's a nice guy.
He's fun. He's kind. He was kind to me when no one else
was. It's . . . this isn't . . . it's just not him. He isn't like that."

Mr. Dace frowned and walked around his desk until he
was standing only a few inches from me. "Are you sure? Do
you know him that well? Because every interaction I've had
with him he's been all those things. He's young. Quick tem-
pered. Immature." He paused and glanced toward the door.
We were still alone. "You aren't. You're more mature than any
seventeen-year-old girl I've met and many twenty-something
females I've known. You have your head on straight. You
have a goal. You're beautiful, smart, and the world is at your
fingertips. Don't waste it on a guy who doesn't see all that."

The kindness and sincerity in his eyes kept me from
defending Nash some more. Instead I said something else.
"You think I'm beautiful now. You didn't see me before." I
was tired of my looks being pointed out. That shouldn't be
the way I was measured.

"No, I didn't. But I wasn't talking about your outward beauty, although there is that. I was talking about what is inside."

Oh. Well . . . Oh.

"Good fight, Coach D," a voice said jokingly, and the moment was gone. Mr. Dace stepped back and turned his attention to the students now entering the room.

"Fighting is never good," he replied, taking his spot behind his desk.

"Maybe not to you, but the rest of us were entertained," another guy said as he dropped his books on his desk.

"I thought Nash was going to go all bad-ass like the good ole Nash we all know and miss. I think he may be coming back to us." That comment came from one of the guys on the football team, I think his name was Eric. I looked at him, but I felt the heat from Mr. Dace's stare and shifted my gaze to meet his.

He didn't have to say anything. I could see the "I told you so" in his eyes.

Was he right? Did I not know Nash at all? Had what I'd seen today been the Nash he once was?

I sat down in my chair and opened the notebook I'd need for class. I didn't listen to any more of the conversation, nor did I look at Mr. Dace. He'd been trying to help me. I understood that. But I didn't want to be warned against Nash. I knew a guy they didn't. I refused to believe the guy I had seen over the years wasn't what I thought he was.

Mr. Dace saw me for who I was, past my clothing size. But he was an adult. It was different. He was mature enough to see past what my body looked like. Although I doubted I'd ever see him dating a fat girl. I should have pointed that out, but I didn't.

Class began, and I took notes. Mr. Dace's eyes lingered on me too long at times, as if he was trying to get a message across to me. I stopped looking up at him. I wasn't giving up on Nash. Not when I had loved him most of my life, and now I had a chance to be with him.

That was if he wasn't angry with me. He'd left upset with me. I worried about it all of class, and I would have texted him if Mr. Dace hadn't been watching me so closely.

The bell seemed to take forever, but when it did ring, I jumped up and hurried for the door. I was almost out of it when Mr. Dace called my name. I paused, wanting to keep going, but he was my teacher, and I knew I couldn't ignore him.

I went back to his desk, and he watched the room until it cleared before looking at me. "I didn't mean to upset you. I just don't want to see you hurt. You deserve better."

I could argue that Nash was special. That I was lucky to

have his attention or interest or whatever it was I had. But I didn't. I wasn't sure I even had that anymore.

"Okay," I said instead.

"If you ever need to talk," he said, and held out a small piece of paper to me.

I reached for it, unsure what it was until it was in my hand. It was a phone number. His phone number. Was that allowed? A teacher giving a student their number to talk?

"Thanks," I said nervously.

"Call me. I'm always available for you."

Again that felt strange. Funny. Like it wasn't exactly meant the way it should be. No, I was overthinking this. Mr. Dace was just being nice. He was concerned, and that was what a good teacher was. Besides, he was gorgeous and had an equally gorgeous girlfriend somewhere, I was sure. I was reading way too much into this.

"Okay, I will," I said, then headed for the door. I needed to find Nash.

Stepping into the crowded hallway, I searched for any sign of him, but he wasn't out here. Neither was Haegan. If I walked to his next period, I'd be late for mine. I debated going to look for him but decided if he wasn't at lunch, I'd go find him then.

"Suspended. Both of them. Three days," I heard someone say in the crowd.

"Fuck," Ryker Lee muttered, and shook his head.

I didn't have to go ask who they meant. I knew.

Mr. Dace had sent them to the office, and they had been suspended.

He'd blame Mr. Dace, although I would argue he'd just been doing his job. I pulled my phone from my pocket and texted Nash on my way to class. By the time I reached the door, he still hadn't responded.

I felt sick. My eyes burned with unshed tears. Quietly I made my way to the back of the room and found a seat. Hopefully, I'd be left alone. Ignored. Like I used to be. I was too close to crying, and I needed to get this day over with.

Maybe Nash would text me back soon. Maybe.

Like the Mature Guy I Was
CHAPTER 28

NASH

Technically, being suspended meant I wasn't supposed to be on school property for three days. I decided I didn't give a shit. I'd left Haegan's house in time to be there when Tallulah walked out of the building. She had texted to check on me, and I had not responded. Simply because I wanted to talk to her face to face. Apologize. I'd let my temper get the best of me, and she was just being sweet Tallulah, worried about me.

When she walked out, I watched her head toward me with her head down. She held her books close to her chest in a defensive way. I could tell she was upset, and I felt guilty now for ignoring her text. I fought the urge to go to her. I needed her to walk to me. I was trying not to be seen. It would just make my suspension worse.

She finally lifted her head to check the parking lot before crossing the lane to where her car was parked. After looking both ways, she paused, and her eyes came back to me. They widened in surprise, then she walked quickly in my direction. I made sure to smile. She needed reassurance. I shouldn't have acted the way I did today with her. Coach D just pissed me off. I hated that man.

The moment I smiled, she walked faster. Relief had taken the place of worry on her pretty face. Damn, I felt guilty about that. I had tried to not think about the fight and telling my parents I was suspended today. Instead, I had focused on observing as Haegan edited his video footage from the past couple of days and made a vlog out of it. I was impressed with how much time he put into it. I also had a main role in this new video. Wasn't sure how that would go, but I went with it.

Now, seeing Tallulah, I knew I'd been selfish just thinking about myself. She deserved a response today. If for no other reason so that she wouldn't worry like she obviously had.

"Hey," she said with a soft nervous voice. I'd done that to her. I was a dick.

I stepped closer and put my hand on her waist, moving her against me slowly before covering her lips with mine. I didn't keep it quick. I tasted her. I didn't care who saw or if anyone was watching. I wanted them to see. This was me making a fucking statement. To Tallulah and everyone else.

Her hands rested on my arms, and I flexed them under her touch. She squeezed, and that only made me flex some more. I was attracted to Tallulah. She made me happy. She reminded me of what was good in this life. She made me want more. Dream of more. With her, football wasn't that important.

The mint on her breath was intoxicating. I didn't want to stop. I could hold her like this, love her like this for hours and never get bored. But I would want more. I wanted more now.

Tallulah had to be the one to end the kiss. I wanted to continue, but if I was caught here, I'd get in trouble. "We need to get you off the property before a teacher sees you," she said in a whisper still close enough that her breath was warm on my skin.

"Leave your car here. Go with me," I said, needing to keep her close.

"Are we going to Haegan's?" she asked. I forgot I'd mentioned that before everything else that happened.

"No, I want you to myself."

Her immediate grin made me want to kiss her again, but she was right. We had to get out of here. If Coach D saw me, he'd be sure I paid for this with more suspension. The man wanted me gone. I wasn't positive, but I had the feeling he liked Tallulah more than a teacher should. The looks he gave her were starting to annoy me. Telling her that, though, would cause a fight. She'd never believe me.

I opened the passenger door and helped her inside. Giving in to my need, I pressed a quick kiss on the corner of her mouth before closing the door and hurrying to get in on my side. We had just pulled out of my parking spot and were headed to the exit when my eyes met Coach D's. He was watching us. Nothing he could do now. He had no proof. Like the mature guy I was, I saluted him, then pulled out onto the main road.

"Who was that?" Tallulah asked.

"Ryker," I lied.

"Oh, I thought he'd be at practice."

"He's headed there now. Guess he saw my truck and wanted to check it out."

I shouldn't have lied. But she wouldn't understand the truth. She liked Coach D. But she was naïve and sweet. She liked everyone. The life she'd lived before her weight loss had kept her in a bubble of sorts. The world around us was fucking ugly. She only saw the happy. The good. Which was unique, considering how she'd been treated before now.

"Where are we going?" she asked.

"My house."

"Oh, do your parents know about today?"

I shook my head. "Not yet. They'll know before they get home from work, though. They always do."

She was silent a moment. I let her think it through.

"Will they be upset I'm there?"

I laughed then. My momma would be upset about a lot of things. But having Tallulah over at my house wasn't one of them. She may call all the ladies in her church prayer circle to tell them the good news. I was dating a girl who wasn't known for her reputation.

"No. They'll be fine with you being there. We will be up in my space above the garage. My dad had the upstairs of the garage finished out this summer for a game room. He was tired of all the noise when my friends were over. We took over his television and living room, so he fixed the situation." The truth was, he had done it to give me an escape. A place of my own. Somewhere for me to recuperate and hopefully lift my spirits. That hadn't happened.

I wasn't supposed to have girls over there without my parents home, but it was Tallulah, and I figured I had a good chance of getting away with it. After the day I'd had, I wanted her alone. We had three hours before my parents got home.

"Wow, that was nice of him."

"It was for his own personal comfort, but yeah, it was nice. The guys enjoy the freedom of being able to curse, sneak beer in, and stay up later than they can at their houses."

She laughed. "I imagine they do," she replied, amused.

I pulled the Escalade into the garage and looked over at her. "We're here."

Most girls would expect to go upstairs and make out. Or straight up have sex. Tallulah was not planning on either. I knew that, and I had to be gentle and patient with her. This was all new to her world, and I liked it. No, I fucking loved it. I wasn't worried about her having any STDs for starters. I'd made Blakely go to the free clinic with me and get checked before I did anything with her. I was safe.

Tallulah opened her door when I did and climbed out. I wanted to spend the next three hours tangled up on the sofa with her. It would make this shit day so much better.

"I wanted you alone for a reason." I was almost warning her.

She turned her head slightly and cut her eyes my way. "I know."

I'd Read Plenty of Books
CHAPTER 29

TALLULAH

I wasn't an idiot. That kiss in the parking lot had been enough to let me know where his head was. I didn't want to be so inexperienced and clueless about these things. I could pretend I wasn't, but that was stupid. Nash knew I was. He knew who I was last year. He knew he'd been my first kiss.

My heart was slamming against my chest so hard I was sure he could hear it as we climbed the stairs in silence leading up to his private den or whatever this was called. My mother would have never approved of one of these. Just like if she knew I was here now, she'd freak out. If I wasn't so excited about being here with Nash, I'd feel bad about betraying her trust in me. But I was almost eighteen.

It wasn't her decision where I went and who I went there with.

He reached around me and opened the door, then held out his hand for me to go inside. It smelled like leather. The lights came on, and there was a large black leather sectional sofa in the center of the room. It didn't just make an L shape; it made two connected in the middle. An ottoman was in the center, and a flat screen hung on the wall. The rest of the space had footballs lining the shelves. Some looked signed and others well used. Framed photos of football players I didn't know decorated the place.

"Wow" was all I could say. They'd really gone all out with this. "I can't imagine why your friends would go anywhere else."

He shrugged. "I haven't been in the best mood this summer. They've been up here a couple times, but only because Ryker forced it on me. The damn footballs remind me of what I lost. I used to collect them. Now they stare at me, taunting me. I need to redecorate. My mom meant well bringing them up here, I guess."

Walking over, I studied the first few balls. They were scribbled on by young kids, or so it appeared from the handwriting.

"Those were our Toy Bowl championship game balls.

We were seven and eight. We signed them. We signed several. I just got those two."

Smiling, I decided these were my favorites. I lifted my head to tell him so when he closed in on me, and my breathing paused. I knew this was coming, just like I knew he planned on more than kissing up here. That didn't make me any less nervous.

"I'd like a good memory up here. So far I haven't had one," he whispered, and I went into his arms willingly. They were strong and warm. He smelled amazing. Being here tucked against him might be the best feeling in the world.

When his lips met mine, I sighed from the pleasure of it all. Being alone up here with him was exciting. My body was tingling, and I shivered as he slid his hands under my shirt. He didn't move up—he simply rested them on my bare back, his fingers slowly caressing my skin.

No guy had ever touched my bare back. That seemed silly, but to me it was a big deal. My hands held on to him, and I felt a little weak. Too many emotions running through me. It was all so new. Overwhelming.

The moment his hands eased upward, I became unable to breathe. I waited as his tongue slid over mine, then I froze with a mix of anxiety and excitement. His thumbs brushed under the bottom of my bra, and I inhaled sharply.

He pulled his mouth back, his eyes locked with mine, and his pupils had gotten so large the color was almost gone. His breathing was heavy as he moved his hands to unclasp my bra.

I gasped when his warm, rough palms touched my breasts. It was different. My entire body seemed to feel it, be affected by it. I was seventeen, and most girls my age had done this long ago. But to me it was exotic.

He closed his eyes a second and inhaled deeply through his nose, then, when he opened them, he looked down at me. "If you want me to stop, I will."

I shook my head. "No," I replied, my voice barely a whisper from my lack of oxygen.

"Lift your arms," he instructed.

I did, knowing why. It was my turn to close my eyes as he took my shirt off. Then tugged my bra until it fell from my arms to the floor. I was topless in front of a guy. In front of Nash. I felt my entire body flush. I knew he'd see it. But at that moment I couldn't care.

"You're beautiful," he said, pulling me back against him. His hands on my back, then tangled into my hair. "I want to feel you like this with nothing between us. Are you okay with that?"

I nodded. Words weren't coming out right now.

He pulled his shirt off quickly, and I only got a glimpse

of his perfectly chiseled stomach before my body was pressed against his. He inhaled with a hiss. "Fuck, that's good." His voice was thick and deep.

I agreed. It was more than good. It was as if a bolt of electricity was humming through me. Every nerve in my body was reacting to this. I wondered if it was always like this, or if this was because it was new to me.

"Lie down with me," he said, moving us toward the sofa. I went, both my hands in his. His eyes were locked on my chest. My breathing making it heave with each deep intake. That seemed to hold his complete attention.

He tugged me down on top of him, and I felt the rigidness under his pants as it pressed into my stomach. I hadn't had sex, but I knew what that was. I also knew why it was like that. I'd read plenty of books. My body stiffened, and he cupped my face with his hand.

"Tallulah, my pants are staying on. This is all I want. To hold you. I promise."

I eased down into the curve of his arm. His left hand slid over my bare breast, and I shivered in response. "Well, I want to hold you and do this," he said, a smile in his voice.

"Okay," I replied, watching his hand on my skin. I squirmed when I felt a tingle between my legs. That was new.

"Unless you want me to touch somewhere else," he said

as he tucked his head in the curve of my neck and inhaled deeply as if smelling me.

I knew that, yes, I wanted his hands somewhere else, but was I ready for that? "I don't know," I said in all honesty.

He moved his right hand to the inside of my thigh and slid it up under my skirt until the side of it touched my panties. I was frozen. My body was screaming for more, but my head was screaming I needed to slow down. This was too much too soon.

"It's okay. I'll leave it like this." His mouth was at my ear, and I shivered.

I wanted to shift my body and move against the hardness in his jeans. But I didn't. I stayed still. As much as I wanted more, I knew for now this was enough.

A knock at the door before it swung open and Ryker's voice calling out "You in here?" was enough to throw the cold water on me I definitely needed. I started to sit up, and Nash moved over me and covered me with his body. "You're topless," he reminded me.

Then he lifted his head to look over the sofa. "Get the fuck out," he growled angrily at Ryker.

"You got a girl in here?" his cousin asked.

"Get. Out!"

Ryker laughed then. "Calm down, I'm going. Thank God you're getting laid. Maybe it'll loosen your ass up some."

"I'm not getting laid," Nash shot back.

Ryker laughed. "I see the bra on the floor. Damn nice size, too."

"I swear to God I am going to beat your ass if you don't get the fuck out of here!"

More laughter. I watched as Nash turned red in the face. He was really upset. Surprisingly, I wasn't. Ryker hadn't seen me. And we had needed something to cool us off. Things had gotten too heated.

"I'm gone. Bye, Tallulah," he called out. Then the door closed.

I stared up at Nash now, worried that Ryker had seen me. But how?

Nash sighed. "It was a good guess. You're the only girl he's seen me with."

Oh. Okay. "But he did see my bra."

Nash smiled then. "Yeah. He did. You worried that he knows what it looks like? He didn't see these," he said teasingly as he brushed a thumb over my left breast.

"True."

We stayed there, staring up at each other a moment. Then another knock on the door sounded. "Your dad just drove up. My guess is he knows about the suspension. Get her shirt on, and I'll come in."

Nash moved fast then. He grabbed my bra and handed

it to me. "Shit," he muttered. "We better hurry."

I quickly got my bra and shirt on while Nash got his shirt on. When he saw I was covered, he went to open the door for Ryker.

Ryker smirked at me. "Glad I called the correct name."

"Don't be a dick," Nash snapped at him.

"I'm saving your ass. You owe me."

Nash looked at me and smiled. It hadn't ended the way I had imagined, but it had been perfect nonetheless.

I've Got Fans All Over the World
Begging for More of You

CHAPTER 30

NASH

I hadn't seen Tallulah since Dad had come home then ordered Ryker to take her home. He'd gotten a call from the principal while at work. I was grounded. He'd even taken my phone and laptop. I'd had no way to contact Tallulah. Which sucked after all we'd done. It hadn't been much by most standards, but with Tallulah it had been a lot. It had been more. Even sex with other girls hadn't been that intimate before.

Walking into school that Tuesday, I was suddenly accosted by females. I froze as girls I'd dated, girls I didn't know, and girls I had previously wanted to know were all around me. Confused, I searched for Tallulah in this mess, but she was nowhere. When I finally took a moment to listen to the chatter all around me, I heard the word *famous*.

Who was famous? Other than Haegan. Were they all over me because I'd been hanging out with Haegan? I'd never been this fucking popular. Hell, not even Brady Higgens had been this popular back when he was at school.

"Welcome back," Haegan said with a slap on my back. "Your appearances on my last two vlogs seemed to be a hit. I've got fans all over the world begging for more of you."

I frowned. "That's what this is about?"

"Oh yeah. There was even a Nash Lee fan club website started up. I saw it last night. Impressive. It took me months to even draw attention. But then I didn't have someone already making it in the business to get me started."

Started? I didn't want to be started.

"Where's Tallulah?" I asked him instead of dealing with my sudden fame. Which seemed weird, and I imagined it would be short lived. I wasn't going to get on a video daily and do crazy shit to get viewers.

"Haven't seen her," he replied. "Did you even watch my vlogs this week?"

I had no interest in watching the vlogs. But that wasn't nice to say, so I replied, "I've been grounded from my phone and computer. I haven't seen anything."

Haegan grinned. "Damn, you're in for a surprise."

"Haegan Baylor," a loud voice called out angrily.

I wasn't sure which one it was since they all looked ready to kill Haegan. But Mr. Dace, Mr. Jones, and both principals stood in front of the office glaring at him.

"Shit. Guess they saw the vlog," he muttered, but was grinning.

"What did you do?" This couldn't have been the fight. He'd edited out so many faces and shit there was no way they could get upset about that.

"I'd guess it was the peanut butter."

"Huh?"

He smirked as if he weren't facing very angry adults who could suspend him yet again. "I covered Dace's piece-of-shit car in peanut butter Friday. Vlogged about it."

Oh shit . . .

"Are you insane?"

He shrugged. "It was funny, Nash. Fucking hilarious."

I watched as he went toward them. He didn't appear worried at all. People were watching and whispering. They'd all seen the vlog, I assumed. He would have gotten away with it if he hadn't vlogged about it.

"I think he's either brilliant or a dumbass," Ryker said, and I turned to see my cousin beside me. "Coach D was pissed Friday, but no one knew who did it. Him ranting and trying to get the door open through the thick-ass peanut butter was priceless. But then yesterday that idiot posted a vlog, and the whole thing was on it. Even him coating the car. Last I checked, it had over two million views already. Two million." He repeated the last part, shaking his head.

I knew Haegan made a lot of money from advertisers and merchandise he sold. The last time I was there, he had boxes of free stuff companies had sent him, wanting him to use it on his vlog. The brand new iPhone no one had yet, a pair of shoes I knew cost over three hundred dollars, and a video game system that didn't release until closer to Christmas. I had been blown away, but he acted like it was no big deal.

"Have you seen Tallulah?" I asked Ryker, changing the subject and getting back to searching the crowd for her. The girls were still there. Would they leave eventually?

"Yeah, she's already gone in her first-period class. She saw that"—he pointed to my unwanted groupies—"and walked away."

Shit.

"Thanks," I said, and excused myself as I walked away from the group and through the few blocking my path. "Excuse me."

"Can we talk?" Blakely asked, stepping in front of me.

"No" was the only response needed for that. I started to move around her.

"Please," she begged, her hand touching my arm. "We need to talk. Maybe after school. Above your garage."

She'd never been up there. We'd been done, or she'd been done with me, by the time it was completed. I didn't like her insinuating I wanted her up there. "Move, Blakely," I replied, annoyed.

"I was dealing with my own problems this summer, Nash. You were too upset over your leg to focus on me. I needed comfort."

I paused then. Stared at her for a moment and decided mentioning how incredibly selfish she had just sounded was pointless. I didn't have time for this. "Yeah, well you got it. Go get some more." I hurried the best I could with my damn leg and finally got free of her. I needed to see Tallulah before I went to my first period.

The classroom was already starting to fill up. I scanned the room when I got to the door and found her two seats from the front. She was reading a book. Others around her were talking and laughing. She seemed oblivious to it all.

"Nash!" some female called out, and I rolled my eyes. This shit was going to have to stop. All this over a damn YouTube video.

Tallulah's head snapped up at my name, and our eyes locked. She looked unsure and hurt. Shit.

I nodded my head for her to come out in the hallway.

She glanced up at the teacher's desk, which was still empty, then stood up and walked my way.

A few other people called out things to me, but I ignored them. I kept my eyes on her. I wanted her to know I was here for her. I didn't want the other attention. She paused at the door, and I stepped out into the hallway.

When I finally had her out there with me, I was relieved but knew I was limited on time. I didn't care about being late to class, but the moment her teacher walked up, she'd go inside.

"My dad grounded me. I've been without any way to communicate. I'm sorry. And that shit with the girls, that was all over some vlogs of Haegan's I was in. I didn't ask for that. I just wanted to see you this morning."

Her smile was small and didn't meet her eyes. "You should probably search yourself online. You're more popular than you realize."

I shrugged. "I don't care. It'll blow over." I reached for her hand. "Come over after school. Please. I've missed you."

She stared at the floor so long I thought she was going to turn me down, but she finally lifted her head and simply nodded. I could live with a nod. For now.

We Were All the Same Inside
CHAPTER 31

TALLULAH

"Tallulah." Mr. Dace called my name just before I left his class. The other students were clearing out quickly, and, if I was honest, I wanted to see Nash, but I couldn't ignore my teacher.

"Yes, sir?" I asked, turning back to face him. He was still sitting at his desk. Today he looked younger than normal. He had on a football T-shirt that fit snugly, like the guys on the team wore, and a pair of jeans with the classic-style Adidas tennis shoes. He could easily pass for a college student.

The girls in the class had noticed too. As if they needed any more of a reason to flirt with him. They all swore they were in love with the man. He was nice. He was a good teacher, and I was thankful to have the teacher's assistant job this semester. It would look good when I applied to colleges this year.

He glanced over my shoulder as the others left the room and waited a moment before responding. Then he moved his gaze back to mine. "Close the door. It's loud out there."

I did as told, then walked back over to his desk. Hopefully this wouldn't take too long.

"I've got three periods' worth of tests to grade, grade logging on the system to do, and study guides that need to be typed up and sent out via e-mail to all the students in all my classes. Then there is football practice. I really need your help after school. I'll give you extra credit points for this. There is no way I am getting it done without you helping me."

I had already worked in here with him during the day. I didn't want to miss my time with Nash after school. We hadn't spent time together since he was suspended. With a sigh, I forced a smile. "Sure. I can work on it all last period and then after school." I might need that extra credit.

Mr. Dace gave me a grin that showcased his dimples. The girls in class loved his dimples. They talked about those all the time too. Most of the time they whispered when they should be doing their classwork. And tugged their shirts down to show off as much cleavage as they could in hopes of getting his attention.

I figured that was why he had asked for me to be his student aid. I didn't sexually harass him.

"Great. I knew you wouldn't let me down. I'll show you everything I need last period. This is a huge help, Tallulah. I can't thank you enough."

I smiled easier this time. I could see Nash after I helped Mr. Dace. He'd understand.

"No problem," I assured him, then finally got to leave the room. It was time for lunch, and the hallways were silent. I'd almost expected Nash to be out here looking for me, but I didn't see him anywhere as I made my way down the hallway toward the closed doors of the cafeteria. The sound from inside could be heard the closer I got. I used to dread walking in those doors, and there was a point that I just wouldn't do it.

I started to smile as I reached them because I wanted to go inside now. I had someone I wanted to see. I belonged. To many, that was something they took for granted. But not me. I never would. I knew what it felt like on the other side.

Squeals and high-pitched screams stopped me just before I went inside. I had just enough time to move out of the way before the door swung open, and a girl with dark brown curls bolted through them still screaming.

She was covered in what appeared to be a blue raspberry slushie from the machine inside the cafeteria. Her hair was saturated with it, and the white polo shirt she wore was blue and dripping as she ran for the restroom across the hall.

Laughter rang out from inside, and I looked in there to see Haegan Baylor in front of it all. With that camera in his hand. That small square thing the teachers hadn't taken from him. It was almost as if they were scared to force him to stop filming in school. He made sure to blur out faces, distort voices, and the like, but it still seemed unfair that he was getting away with it.

Haegan winked at me with that annoying amused grin of his. Had he done that? Surely he hadn't? If someone had actually poured a slushie on her, they'd be in the office with a ticket home for several days.

"Where you been?" Nash asked, pulling my thoughts off of Haegan and the slushie.

"Mr. Dace needed me," I said, then pointed toward the restroom. "What happened?"

Nash looked like he was trying not to grin. "Paige got spooked. Thought the rubber snake Haegan put under the slushie machine was real. No one else had noticed it, but she saw it just as she finished getting her drink and screamed, tossing the slushie in the air. Damn thing went all over her."

I didn't think this was funny, nor did I see why he did. "Why would Haegan put a rubber snake there?" I asked, already knowing the answer.

Nash shrugged. "He does shit like that. Pranks and the like for his vlog. Gets more viewers. People laugh. It's why he's famous."

He was famous because he humiliated people? "That's terrible."

Nash frowned. "She'll get to go home early. It's just a slushie. Won't kill her."

No, she'd survive. But the whole student body would remember. The world would see it on his vlog. And she would be humiliated because, although her face wasn't seen, the kids here would know it was her.

"Have you ever been the one everyone laughed at? Do you know how it feels to hear laughter directed at you? Ever been humiliated?" I shook my head for him. "No, you haven't."

"Aw, come on Tallulah. It wasn't that big of a deal."

Not to him. Not to Haegan or any of these other insensitive people still snickering and mimicking her. But to her it was. It would be. She'd never forget it.

"I need to go help Mr. Dace. He's got some work for me. I'll be late after school, helping him get things caught up," I said, and turned to walk to the restroom. I was going to see if I could help the girl.

"What about after school? My house?" Nash called out.

"I'll stop by when I'm done."

He didn't look okay with that. But I didn't care. Right now I was being reminded of the guy who laughed at me last May. The guy who found humor in my pain. I didn't like that guy. I liked the one from the water tower. But was that even who Nash was?

"Fine. Go help Coach Douchebag. See if I give a fuck!" Nash called out, then stalked off as if I wasn't there. He didn't give me a chance to respond. But what would I say?

I was seeing a Nash I wanted to believe didn't exist. The guy who had been kind to me since elementary school, that was the one I was falling in love with. But this Nash . . . I didn't think I could even like him.

Going inside the restroom, I heard the sobs immediately. My chest hurt. I didn't know the girl. I'd seen her before. She had a big group of friends. She was in the band. This wasn't something she had experienced, until now.

I walked over and got some paper towels. "I can help you get it out of your hair. Then we can get you to the office before they all leave the cafeteria, and you can go home."

Paige looked up at me with red-rimmed eyes and nodded. "Thank you."

In that moment I saw myself. We were all the same inside. Didn't matter how we looked or who our friends were. We all wanted the same thing. To belong. To be accepted.

Jesus, You're a Buzzkill
CHAPTER 32

NASH

I could hear them talking, and Tallulah laughed at something the dickhead said. She was enjoying her time in there. She wasn't at all concerned about missing our afternoon together. Why wasn't he at fucking football practice? It was after three. He should have left her by now. I was coming to talk to her, apologize about earlier. She had been right. The slushie thing hadn't been funny.

"Are you stalking them now?" Haegan asked behind me. I turned my head to look at him and saw that damn camera.

"Get that off me," I grumbled, then looked back into the classroom. Coach D was leaning over her, pointing at something on the computer screen in front of her. He was too close. If any other teacher saw that, they'd agree it was out of line. The man liked Tallulah. He was keeping her here so she wouldn't be with me.

"Looks like we have a student-teacher romance a-brewing," Haegan whispered. He then moved closer with the camera.

"I said to turn that off," I snapped.

He smirked. "You said to get it off you. Not turn it off. Besides, this could end up being the world's best blackmail. Do you know the grades I could get from this? Stellar, my friend. Stellar fucking grades." Haegan moved closer to the window in the door.

I didn't want either of them to see us. Especially Tallulah. She was already mad at me, and seeing Haegan there with the camera wasn't going to help. "Seriously, move. I don't want her to see you."

He ignored me. "I think he's going to make a move. You want to go in there and throat punch him? Would make fantastic vlog material."

I shoved him out of their view. "Stop it," I warned. I wasn't protecting the slimy-ass teacher who needed to date girls his own age and leave mine alone. I was doing it for Tallulah. She was so naïve she had no idea what was happening. She truly thought she was there to help the man.

"Jesus, you're a buzzkill." He finally lowered the camera and turned it off. "Fine. If you don't want to get this on video, let's go find something more interesting to do. Watching them dance around each other is boring if I'm not getting to record it."

I started to tell him to leave. I wasn't going anywhere with him. His dumbass rubber snake had caused me to miss time with Tallulah. Haegan wasn't going to ruin this for me. His life revolved around that camera. After seeing the shit he owned and finding out how much money he made from it, I understood. But I didn't want that. I just wanted her.

Coach D bent his knees and dropped to his haunches until he was eye level with her. She turned her head to look at him, and he was saying something very serious. Her brow furrowed, but she was listening. This did not look like her helping him. Nothing about grading papers was this serious.

His hand went up and cupped her face, and I took a step toward the door. Haegan's hand was on my arm immediately. "Wait. Don't go in there yet," he said in a quiet voice beside me. If he had that fucking camera out again, I was going to break it.

Coach D leaned in closer, and I couldn't tell if he was talking or not, but he sure as hell looked like he was about to kiss her. Going in there and stopping it was my first reaction, but I paused. Because Tallulah wasn't moving away. She wasn't leaning closer, but she wasn't moving back, either. Would she let him do this? Did she like this man? Had I been missing something all along?

"Oh, snap," Haegan muttered just as Coach D closed the space between them. I was frozen. Unable to speak. Move. Or breathe.

"Holy mother, why did I turn off my good camera? This watch camera isn't going to be as good, but it'll do." He continued talking. I just stood there. In a horror film or nightmare, watching it but not believing it.

Then I began walking. Away from it. Away from what all I'd seen. Tallulah wasn't that girl. She didn't kiss teachers. We weren't exclusive, I guess. Or were we? Hell, I wasn't used to good girls. I didn't know what Tallulah considered exclusive. But in my head she had been mine. I'd had her topless in my arms. Didn't that mean something to her? Could I have been wrong? Was this thing we had a joke? Tallulah getting her revenge? Had she fucking played me? All that sweet-and-kind shit couldn't have been an act. But then I was a cripple. She was gorgeous. Why would she have chosen me?

"We aren't gonna stay to see if they do more? He might fuck her on the desk. Your revenge could be getting his ass thrown in jail."

I didn't respond to that. But my entire body tensed. My chest hurt. My head was pounding. Everything I thought was . . . wasn't. Tallulah wasn't what I thought. She was in there kissing a fucking teacher. She wasn't even cheating on me with a guy our age. She was with a teacher. Fucking hell!

"I need to get smoked. I know you have some," I said as I shoved the door open and stalked out of the school.

"You want weed? Really?" Haegan sounded excited. As if his world was full of sunshine and rainbows. Seeing Tallulah making out with a teacher hadn't twisted his gut.

I went directly to his Porsche. It was new, completely loaded, and he'd paid cash for it. All because of that camera he had all the time. The lights blinked, and I jerked open the passenger door, then climbed in.

Once he was inside, he reached over, opened the glove compartment, and there for anyone to find was a bag of weed. "Let's get baked." It wasn't a suggestion. He was serious. And I decided so was I.

"In the school parking lot?" I asked, looking around, although the windows were tinted and no one could see us.

"There's a student-teacher make-out session going on in that building. Do you honestly think us smoking a little is gonna be the main concern here?"

Being reminded of what I'd seen, I nodded. "Fine, but you want to smoke that in this car?"

He inhaled deeply and then laughed. "Take a deep one, dude. It's been smoked in here many times before."

He was right. I'd been too upset to think about how his expensive-ass car smelled when I'd gotten inside. Apparently he wasn't worried about resell value or his mother taking a whiff. "What if your mom gets in this car and smells this?" My parents would kill me.

He just chuckled and went to rolling up a smoke. On the freaking dashboard. Of a Porsche. He was insane.

"I bought her house. What the fuck you think she's gonna say?"

Wow. I hadn't realized that.

"You first," he said, handing it to me once it was ready.

I looked at it only a moment, then decided what the hell and took it.

He Doesn't Know How to Love
CHAPTER 33

TALLULAH

After the complete shock of what had just happened sunk in, I jumped up, tripping over the chair I had been sitting in, and moved back. Away. Far away. Had that really just happened? I'd been laughing with Mr. Dace about his bad computer skills; then he was down here beside me telling me how much he appreciated me. I had felt a little uncomfortable by the closeness.

He had touched my face and told me I was beautiful. He said he wished he was younger or that I was older. I had no words and wanted to leave just as his mouth covered mine. This was definitely not okay.

"I'm sorry. I didn't mean to scare you. I just . . . I

think about you all the time. I can't get you out of my head." He was talking again. Saying things that I couldn't believe. He was my teacher. This wasn't right.

I shook my head and backed up, then decided I better run. He called out my name as my hands opened his door frantically. My heart was pounding in my chest, and tears stung my eyes. I realized I was scared. I wasn't sure of what. He had just kissed me, but I was new to all this. To guys being attracted to me. I wasn't ready to have a grown man's attention. I didn't want it. Had I done something to make him think I did?

I stumbled out of his room after fumbling with the door in my panicked state.

"Tallulah!" He called out my name again, but I kept running. I'd left my book bag behind. In his room. My keys were in that bag. I had no way to get home. A tear rolled down my face, and I kept running. I had no idea where I was going to run. So I turned and ran into the women's restroom.

Stopping at the sink, I grabbed it for support and looked at the wide-eyed scared girl in the mirror. What had happened today? How had things gone from good to this? Was this my fault? Had I made Mr. Dace think this was okay? That I wanted it?

I didn't even have my phone. It, too, was in my backpack. I was without anything. I couldn't call . . . Nash.

That's who I wanted to call. That's who I wanted to run to. But I had no way to call or leave. I was stuck.

The door to the restroom opened, and I spun around to see Mr. Dace standing there. He looked upset. He had his hands in the front pockets of his jeans and didn't look scary or intimidating at all.

I backed up anyway. "This is the ladies' restroom." I pointed out the obvious.

"I'm sorry, Tallulah. I shouldn't." He paused and ran a hand over his face with a sigh. "That was wrong. I don't have an excuse for it. I sure as hell didn't mean to scare you."

Well he had. "Why did you do it?" I blurted out, then backed up more. I wanted distance.

He lifted his head, and his eyes were sad. He seemed lost. In pain. Lonely. "Because I'm in love with you. I've fought it since day one. The first time I saw you. But you're impossible to resist. I can't help how my heart feels."

I shook my head no. "Mr. Dace," I said.

"Jack. Please . . . my name is Jack. I want to hear you call me by my name."

Was he serious? This wasn't okay. Why me? I never acted like I wanted this. Did I?

"Mr. Dace," I said, refusing to say his first name. "I don't think you know me enough to love me."

He chuckled softly. "What do you know about love,

Tallulah? You're so damn innocent. I've watched you, studied you, been fucking fascinated with you from the moment you walked into my room. So yes, sweetheart, I know that I love you. There is no question in my mind."

I wasn't that naïve. Love took time. It took knowing someone. It took a lot more than thinking you know them because you have observed them. Like with Nash. I thought I loved him before. But I hadn't known him really.

I did now.

And . . . I knew I loved him. Even with his flaws. I had my own set of flaws. No one was perfect. Nash would make mistakes, just like I would. It didn't make me love him less.

"He flirts with other girls all the time. When you aren't watching, he looks at them. He doesn't know how to love. Teenage boys never do. They need to grow up first. Don't give your heart to a guy who can't cherish it. Because yours is special. So incredibly special."

What was he talking about? Had I said I loved Nash out loud?

"He will hurt you again and again if you let him. I see how you look at him. It makes me insane with jealousy. If he understood what he had, he wouldn't be running around with that other kid trying to become famous. He wants a life out of here. He lost his football future, and he's working on making a new one. You're not in that life, Tallulah. You're just the girl from high school. The one he likes. The one who's prettier than the others. The one who makes him feel important again. But you are so much more than that." He took a step toward me, and I had nowhere else to back up to this time. But I didn't need to. He wasn't going to attack me.

He was just trying to warn me. About things I needed to hear. I didn't know boys. He was right. I was naïve. Innocent. Clueless. And loving Nash was probably a mistake.

"I don't want to lose you. I won't touch you again . . . if you don't want me to. But don't pull away from me. Please." His voice was strained.

I found it odd he wasn't begging me not to say anything. Or to keep it a secret because he would lose his job. That didn't seem to be his concern. I was his concern. I didn't want it to, but that made me feel special. It was warped, but I still felt important. As if losing me was harder than losing his job.

"I need to get my backpack from your room and go home. This, I don't know how to deal with this. Just give me time to think it through. Maybe see if I can understand it."

He stepped back and gave me a small nod. "Sure. Whatever you need. I'm here. If you want me to be."

I was going to have to walk past him to get to the door. I didn't think he was going to reach out and grab me, but I was stiff and nervous anyway as I made my way to the door. The hallway was empty, and I turned to look back at him. "It's clear." I wasn't protecting him as much as I was protecting me. I didn't want a rumor started about me in the restroom with a teacher.

"If you need me, Tallulah, you can always call."

I simply nodded and went to get my things. I was never going to call Mr. Dace. That much I was sure of. I might want to work on getting tougher in order to not fall apart when Nash did hurt me, but I wasn't going to get Mr. Dace to help me. I was going to keep my distance. This was wrong, and I hadn't asked for it. I had thought he was a good teacher. I'd completely misunderstood his intentions. I was so naïve.

Pausing, I glanced back at him. "You know there are about ten other girls easily that would have been a better choice. They'd have wanted your attention."

He gave me a sad smile. "I didn't want to love a student. But we can't control our heart."

CHAPTER 34

NASH

Getting lit was probably the worst idea I'd had in a long time. But I was. We were. Lit, that is. And to make it worse, I was in the passenger side of a Porsche with an equally lit driver. Shit. We'd go to fucking jail if we were pulled over. If not jail, then my dad would just murder me with his bare hands. That made me laugh. The image of Dad strangling me to death.

Why was that so damn funny?

"Nothing like a blunt to make you feel better."

I had to agree, although this was still stupid. I just couldn't seem to care at the moment. Life wasn't so bad. The image of Tallulah kissing the fucking coach, however, wasn't funny. Not even after several drags off that blunt.

"Can't believe she did it," I said in response.

He held the blunt back out to me. "Jesus, man. Take some more. Let that shit go."

I looked at it, thought about it, then shook my head no. I'd had enough already. No amount of weed was going to make me laugh at what I'd seen.

"Where are we going?" I asked, ignoring the blunt.

"Fuck if I know" was his response. Then he chuckled and took another pull from it. "You need more. You're scowling again."

He was looking over at me. Not the road and that made me nervous. Maybe I did need more to lighten up. "Watch the fucking road," I snapped.

He rolled his eyes. "Never knew a guy who could smoke the good stuff and be so damn uptight still. Where's your humor? We need to go do something for the vlog. What about we go buy a shit ton of eggs and go egg el douchebag's house?"

Although the idea of egging Coach D's house was tempting, putting it on a vlog would only get us caught. "We'll have to pay for it. He can file charges when the evidence is on the vlog."

Haegan shrugged. "So."

So? The guy was either too damn high or crazy. Either way, he was driving this car, and I might need to wear my seat belt. I quickly snapped it on. He saw me and laughed. Loudly.

"You don't want a police record. Fine. I got a better idea." He was still laughing as he said it.

"What's your idea?" I asked, not sure I'd be participating.

"You scared of chickens?"

"Chickens?" I asked for clarity.

"Yep. Motherfucking chickens."

I shrugged. "No. Who's scared of chickens?"

He smirked. "My mom. She's terrified of them."

I wasn't sure where this idea was going. "And?"

"And I know where I can get about five chickens. Going to borrow them, take them home. Leave them in the kitchen and pour some oil behind me on the floor. Set up a camera. Mom come's home, walks into the kitchen, slips and falls on her ass as the chickens go crazy, and she shits herself screaming." He is laughing so hard now he has his eyes closed.

"Watch the damn road!" I yelled.

He sped up and shot me a grin. "You need another smoke. Seriously."

I heard the horn then. It was loud, the tires screeching almost sounded like screams. Haegan yelled "FUCK!" and then the clash of the two vehicles slammed so hard my body jerked violently against the seat belt. It took my breath. Pain shot up my right arm, and the dash felt like it was in my lap. I inhaled deeply once I got my breath. The smell of burnt rubber filled the air. I shook my head trying to clear it and felt the pain there, too. Reaching up, I touched something wet and took my hand away to see blood covering my fingers. I was bleeding.

Then I turned to see if Haegan was bleeding. If he was hurt. "You okay?" I asked.

He didn't move. His head was turned the other way, and he seemed limp. "Haegan, man? You good? I think my head's bleeding."

Still no response. Nothing. My stomach dropped. I reached over to touch him, knowing before I did it what I would find. I shook his arm and his head fell forward, but not before I saw his eyes. Open and vacant. No life there.

"HAEGAN!" I yelled his name, but I knew he couldn't hear me.

"NASH!" Someone yelled my name. "IS THAT YOU IN THERE? ARE YOU OKAY?" That voice belonged to my uncle Anthony.

"Yes, sir, but . . . but Haegan isn't," I called back out to him.

"STAY STILL. PARAMEDICS ARE ON THEIR WAY! DON'T MOVE. OKAY?"

"Yes, sir," I replied. I couldn't move even if I wanted

to. I was pinned in. This all seemed unreal to me. Haegan wasn't really dead. This shit didn't happen. We weren't even going that fast. Were we? I tried to turn my head to see out the window, but it was crushed against something. Glass was in my lap, and I saw my arm was cut in several places. I hadn't noticed that before. My head was pounding now. It was harder to keep my eyes open.

Haegan was limp. His chest wasn't rising and falling. There was nothing. I'd never seen death before. Saw life go out of eyes like that. It was haunting. He'd just been laughing. Loving his life. His money, cars, fame. He was never sad or depressed. The guy was always smiling or smirking.

But not now. It was all gone. Did souls exist? Did his just leave his body and take all that with him? Seemed so basic to just have organs that shut down and with that took the life. There had to be more, didn't there? Something inside that left when the body was no longer usable.

I heard my uncle calling my name again, but I was weak. Tired. I was also scared that if I closed my eyes, the soul inside me could escape. I didn't want the vacancy staring out of me when my uncle got to me. This decision to get in a car and smoke weed had been not only stupid but fatal. It had been selfish. I had been selfish. Worried about me. Not about what could happen and who it would affect.

"NASH!" My uncle called out again. I tried to reply,

but my voice was too quiet. I reached over to knock on something, but I didn't have the energy.

I was slowly fading out when I felt the car shift. Heard the creaking of metal being moved. Then light came in, and the first face I saw was Uncle Anthony's just before I gave up and closed my eyes.

"Stay with us, Nash," a voice that I didn't recognize called out to me. I fought against the pull of sleep, but my eyes wouldn't open. I just nodded my head. Let them know I was there. Awake.

"Do you know this one?" the same voice asked.

"It's the new kid. Haegan Baylor, I believe. He does the Internet video stuff. I've heard Ryker talk about him."

The other voice sighed. "We need to find his parents. He's gone."

I knew that, but hearing someone else confirm it made it real. This wasn't a dream. This was life. One that Haegan no longer got to live in. All the things he'd accomplished, and it was gone. Just that easily.

This Was All a Bad Dream

CHAPTER 35

TALLULAH

Lights flashed everywhere. Ambulances, police cars, and fire trucks blocked the street, while cars were parked lining the street, filling the grocery parking lot and the post office. It seemed most of the town was here. Outside watching. We couldn't see much. But we all knew.

That Porsche was the most expensive thing in this town. It belonged to one person. We hadn't known the passenger had been Nash until Ryker showed up on the scene. His truck had come to a screeching halt, and he'd jumped out running.

Ryker had been let through the barricade. Then Nash's father and mother had also shown up together. His mother crying as his father held her close to his side. They were then let through. But that had been it. No one else.

So we all waited. No one had shown up for Haegan. Did that mean he was okay? Was it Nash who was injured? His family wasn't leaving. Sirens were still going off, the lights still flashing. But the onlookers were silent. I had been leaving school when I drove up on it. The ambulances were already here then. I hadn't known who or what had happened.

It had been after I parked that I saw the Porsche and the old model Lincoln Continental that were smashed together. The Porsche suffering much more damage than the older larger car. I heard others talking. It belonged to Mrs. Wise, the Baptist minister's wife.

The time seemed to pass so slowly as I waited. For something. Any news. When my mother's arm slipped around my waist, I jumped. I hadn't seen her drive up. "You okay?" she asked me, kissing the side of my head.

"No. But how I am isn't what's important."

"Yes, Tallulah, it is."

I started to argue when we heard it. The sirens came back to life. An ambulance was moving. The road cleared immediately as everyone watched it speed off toward the nearest hospital. Cops were holding people back.

The next car that arrived was let inside the secure area. Mom squeezed me tightly. She inhaled quick and loud.

"What is it?" I asked, feeling my panic on the verge of exploding. I'd been holding it together, but something about the look on her face made me fear that the world as I knew it was about to change forever.

"It's okay," she said, but her face didn't echo her words. It was fearful, worried, pained.

"Mom, who was that?" I demanded, pulling away from her.

She turned her gaze to me. Unshed tears glistened there. "Norton Hill. The coroner."

My stomach turned, and I became ill. Stepping over into the grass, I bent at the waist and began to heave. Everything I'd eaten that day came back up. I felt my mom's hand on my back and heard the sob from her mouth.

This was all a bad dream. One I wanted to wake up from now. Right this instant. I hated this. My knees felt weak, and I stood up, taking the tissue Mom held out for me and wiping my face.

"We don't know who he's here for," she said, but it didn't matter. Did it? Someone was dead. Someone didn't make it. I wanted to believe that in my heart I would feel the same no matter whose life had been taken in that crash. But I knew the truth. I didn't want it to be Nash. I tried to breathe and couldn't.

"There's Ryker," she said, nodding her head as he

walked back to his truck. I wanted to run to him. To ask him about Nash. But I was terrified. I took a step in his direction, and he lifted his gaze to meet mine.

He paused and nodded. "He's okay. He was the one in the ambulance."

Those words. I had stood here almost an hour not knowing. Living in a state of hope and fear. Afraid my nightmare was going to get worse. But he was okay. Nash was okay.

My knees started to give out then, and my mother was there. I fell into her arms, and a sob broke free as I let out all the emotion I'd been holding in. I sobbed in relief that I hadn't lost him. That he wasn't gone. His life was here. I should have cried for whoever didn't make it. I should have prayed for their family. But in that moment all I could do was cry tears of relief.

I heard my mother thank him. I couldn't say anything. She didn't ask who the coroner was here for. It was a truth that no one wanted to face.

"They're taking him to Mercy. It's twenty minutes further but he's stable, and they are better equipped if he needs any surgery," Ryker said.

He was stable. That made me cry harder.

"Thank you. Once she's calm, we will drive that way," Mom replied.

"I understand," he replied.

"Ryker! Are Nash and Haegan okay?" a female voice called out.

"Nash is" was his response, then I heard a car door close. His engine started, and I stood there, slowly letting that sink in. He hadn't said Haegan was okay. Pulling back, I looked at the scene now becoming clearer as the other ambulance left. The lights weren't on, but it had a body inside.

"Ohmygod! He didn't say Haegan was," the girl screamed hysterically. I ignored her. That dramatic response was meant to draw attention to herself.

"Do you think he's . . . dead?" I asked my mother in a whisper. I hated even saying the words.

She didn't look like she wanted to answer that. "I don't know."

"The other ambulance left without their lights on," I pointed out.

"We don't know about Mrs. Wise, either. Or if someone was in her car."

I saw a family standing together crying. An older man I recognized as the Baptist church minister held a woman and three young kids close as they all sobbed. He looked sad. Broken. I didn't need to be told why. The scene was obvious. Heartbreakingly so.

"I don't think she lived," I said, the words heavy in my chest.

"Me either," Mom agreed.

The family had lost someone today. Someone they loved very much. What if I had lost someone? What if that had been my mom's car?

"Haegan Baylor is gone! No!" a girl wailed behind us. Others joined her.

"Let me drive," Mom said as she took my arm, and we walked back to her car. "We can come get yours later."

I didn't want to drive right now so I made no argument.

Blakely was doubled over, sobbing in a group of friends. There had been no word on Haegan yet. But the town seemed to already believe he was gone.

I remembered the night I met him at the game. He'd been annoying and full of himself. But he was important to a lot of people. He had a family, friends, fans. All of who would mourn him. A void would be left in his family's life, one that could never be filled.

Tears filled my eyes again as I climbed into my mother's car. This time for the loved ones left behind.

You Have a Crowd Waiting
on You Out There

CHAPTER 36

NASH

My mother paced in front of my bed, wringing her hands, and my dad sat in the chair beside the bed they had me lying on, with his elbows resting on his knees and his head hanging down, staring at the floor. I was alive. That had been the most important thing at first. But after, the doctor came in to inform us that I had tested positive for marijuana and they expected the same from Haegan's evaluation. Mrs. Wise's husband could press charges. I was eighteen now.

We were all waiting for the hospital to release me. Dad had called a lawyer. I'd heard him talking to him. I hadn't been driving, so it sounded like it wouldn't be as severe as it could have been. They didn't know what to say to this. I could apologize for my stupidity. But those were words. They did no good. They didn't change anything.

Haegan was dead. Mrs. Wise was dead. I had six stitches in my head, a broken arm, and some bruising and cuts. Nothing more. I'd walk out of here today. Life would go on. My parents were upset over the weed and the fact I could be prosecuted as an adult.

I had just seen my friend die. Looked into his lifeless eyes. Saw a family grieving over a woman they loved, a woman they lost. I deserved whatever happened. I had lived. I wasn't worried about what they decided to do with me. I had made a mistake that had altered lives.

There was a knock on the door, and Ryker stepped inside. "They gonna let you out of here anytime soon?" he asked. He didn't know about the weed yet. He probably had guessed it, though.

"Yes, soon," I told him.

"You got a waiting room out there full of people. I told them you'd be getting out soon. No reason to come in here and visit. But Tallulah is out there with her mom. Thought you'd want to see her."

Tallulah.

The reason I'd smoked the weed. That motherfucking kiss. If I hadn't seen her kiss Coach D, I would have seen her tonight. I wouldn't have gotten messed up, and Haegan would be alive. Mrs. Wise would be alive.

"I don't want to see her. She can go on home." The words came out hard. Angry. I felt all three pairs of eyes on me. I didn't meet any of them. I turned my heated glare to the window and wished I'd never met her. Never kissed her. Never spoken to her.

"You sure about that?" Ryker asked, confused.

"Yes, I'm sure," I snarled.

"Well, all righty then." He was confused, but he wasn't going to push me for a reason, at least not yet. The only other person who knew about the kiss she'd had with Coach D was gone. I held that information. No one else did. I had the power to hurt her and ruin him. But I wasn't sure I could do it. Not because I was concerned for him. It was her. She'd be humiliated. She'd be faced with legal issues and questions. She would get attention she didn't want.

"Give us a minute, Ryker," my dad said, standing up.

Ryker nodded and went back out into the hallway. Once the door closed behind him, Dad cleared his throat to get my attention. I didn't want to talk, but I turned to him.

"The girl, is she into drugs? Is that how this got started?"

I laughed. It wasn't a real laugh. It was hollow, empty. "No."

"Then why are you so angry with her? The moment Ryker mentioned her, you tensed and changed. If she had something to do with this, we need to know. This is important, son."

I swung my legs off the bed and stood up to get away from him. I needed distance. I wasn't talking about Tallulah with him. For now her secret would be her secret. It would be one that ruined me. Ruined many lives.

"She's a bitch. A lying, manipulative bitch. That's all. But she's never in her life touched weed or even a damn beer."

My mother sighed. "Then why weren't you with her? Why did you have to spend time with that boy?"

Hearing Haegan referred to as "that boy" felt wrong. Like his life hadn't been important. Like it hadn't made an impact. I loved my mother, but sometimes she only saw what affected her.

"He was someone's son, big brother, and he was loved by fans all over the world. He was a friend that helped me get out of a funk and taught me that I could find life outside of football. He was crazy as hell, did insane shit, but he was fun. So don't call him 'that boy,' Mom. He was Haegan. Today I was listening to him laugh, plan a prank with chickens, and then I saw his eyes empty. Void. The life gone. Just like that. Just . . . like . . . that." I walked over to the window and put both palms flat on the cool glass. There was a life out there. It didn't stop because others died.

It kept going, yet it wouldn't be the same.

"I didn't mean he wasn't important. I was just saying Tallulah was a better influence."

Shaking my head, I wondered what Mom would think if I told her Tallulah was making out with our literature teacher. What kind of influence was that?

"Mom, I've smoked weed before. I didn't know Haegan then. He didn't force it on me. I am a big boy. It was a choice I made. A mistake that I can't take back. It's done, and I've got to live with it. Haegan's family has to live with it. Pastor Wise and his family have to live with it."

"Nash! Son, when did you start doing drugs? We've taught you better than that. I trusted you. We both did." My mother was upset over me smoking weed. Great. I got her problem with it, but there was a bigger issue.

"I don't think he's confessing to being an addict, babe," Dad said, trying to calm her down. "He's just pointing out that Haegan isn't to blame for this. Nash is grown. He made his own choices, and he is owning up to that."

Mom let out a sob, and he went over to her. Pulled her to his chest. My eyes met his, and I saw the disappointment there, but I also saw the relief. I was here. Alive. It could have been me. They weren't saying it. But I knew they were thinking it.

The door opened, and the nurse walked in. "We've got your release papers. Looks like you have a crowd waiting on you out there."

She was trying to be happy and upbeat. That was her job, I guess. But I didn't want to go out and face any of them. I wanted to go home. Alone.

"I don't want to deal with any of that," I told my dad.

He nodded. "I'll go clear them out."

"But that's rude," my mother said, looking stressed.

Dad paused. "He needs time. He watched a friend die today. Give him some time. Being polite isn't what's important now."

Mom sniffled and nodded her head. "You're right," she agreed. "Send them home, but thank them for coming."

Dad had been planning on just that. I had no doubt. But Mom needed to say it anyway.

When he left, the nurse started to tell me how to take care of my stitches, but I didn't hear any of it. My thoughts were somewhere else.

CHAPTER 37

TALLULAH

Ryker was frowning as he walked into the waiting room. His gaze scanned the crowd until it landed on me. The frown grew deeper as he made his way toward where Mom and I were standing. I'd chosen a spot near the window. Away from everyone else. I needed air. They were all packed together, going over what they had heard or seen. I didn't want to recap it. My stomach stayed in knots, and that made it worse.

"Hey," Ryker said, and shifted feet. He seemed uncomfortable.

"Is he okay?" I asked, worried something had changed. Wishing I could see him just to reassure myself he was alive.

"Yeah, uh, he's upset. He saw Haegan, after he was gone. He saw it all. It's haunting him, messing with his head."

I'd never seen someone die before. I imagined it was the worst experience one could go through. "Can I see him?" I asked.

Ryker sighed, then shook his head. "No. He . . . he . . . doesn't want to see you. He is angry with you. I don't know what went down with y'all before all this happened, but he's adamant that you leave."

I stood there confused and in shock. We'd argued a little about my helping Mr. Dace. It hadn't been a real fight. I hadn't left angry with him. Not that kind of angry. I was disappointed. But it hadn't made me not want to see him again.

"I don't understand," I whispered.

Ryker shrugged. "Like I said. Not sure what happened, but he needs space and time. Can't force him to see you if he doesn't want to."

That was it? I was just supposed to leave. Go away and give him time. He didn't want to see me. That knowledge made my already fragile heart crumble. Today had been one I would never forget and would have nightmares about for years to come. Mr. Dace, then the car accident, then this.

"Let's go, honey." Mom's hand was on my arm. I

realized her small touch was much-needed support. I wanted to ball up on the floor and cry. About so many things. But I couldn't. Not here.

I nodded my head and let her begin to lead me away. But I stopped and turned to look back at Ryker. "I loved him, you know." I started to say more and stopped. That was something I hadn't truly admitted to myself. I had claimed I'd been in love with him most of my life, but until I got to know him, I hadn't understood what really loving a guy meant. I did now. And even though his rejection was ripping me apart, I would forgive him. That's what love did.

Ryker's expression was pained. He didn't say more. I left then. Walked away not looking back. Not searching for signs of Nash in the hallway. Mom led me outside, where the sun still shined. The warmth of the afternoon was still heavy in the air. My mom's car was there, parked where we left it. Everything was the same, but it was also very different.

When we were both inside, she reached over and squeezed my hand. "He will regret this. But he is in pain right now. Ryker's right. He needs space, and if he doesn't see how you could help him heal, then that is his loss."

No. His loss was his friend. I was just a girl he was spending time with. Where I had fallen in love so easily, he hadn't. He had been my first kiss. I had been one of his many. I understood it, yet it didn't make it hurt less. This was a growing pain. Nash had taught me a lot. More than I realized I needed to know. Being invisible and alone with my books had been easier. I had hurt when I was made fun of or left out, which was daily. But I'd never felt this sharp pain in my chest. It made it hard to breathe.

The saying "It is better to have loved and lost than to have never loved at all" didn't seem true to me. I disagreed. I thought it would be easier to not know how it felt for your heart to break. There was no going back. I knew now.

"He was the first boy I loved. I feel as if I will always love him, but this . . . this pain I will never forget. I understand now why you never married. When I was a little girl, I daydreamed about you meeting a man and how beautiful you would be as a bride. I'd get a daddy, and we'd have a family photo on the wall with a dog. A large yellow lab." I hadn't thought of that dream in a long time. I'd outgrown it years ago. "But I am glad you didn't. I am glad it was just us. That your heart was never broken. That you were happy the way we were."

My mother sighed. I didn't look her way. I kept staring out the window as we drove back to Lawton. I knew when I said it she wouldn't like it. But it was true. She'd been smart to hide from love, to not try to find it.

"Tallulah," she said, her voice heavy with what sounded

like regret. "That's not how I want you to feel. I never married again because no man was the right one. I wasn't looking for just me but you, too. If I were to fall in love with a man, he'd have to love you as his own. That would be the final piece to winning my heart. No man I dated was ever good enough to be your father. I had expectations, and not one man I dated met those. That's why I never married."

She had hardly dated. I could remember only two men in the past she'd brought home to meet me. "You didn't look very hard, then. Because you've only dated twice in my life."

Mom laughed softly. I turned this time to look at her. I didn't know why that was funny. I used to feel sad for her. Worry that she was lonely without a husband. She didn't take her eyes off the road. "Oh, sweetheart. Only two men made the cut to get to meet you. Out of the many, many men I dated, the two you met I went out with several times and trusted that they just might possibly be good enough for you. They were good men, or I'd never have brought them to meet you. But in the end I realized I wasn't one hundred percent sure that they were what you needed. What we needed."

My mom had dated many, many men? What? "You dated how many men exactly?" I asked, still shocked by this news.

She shrugged. "Gosh, I don't know. Friends would fix

me up on blind dates. Those never went well. I met other men at work. I had many dates that never made it past the first one. Dating for me was like an interview. I think it's that way with all single moms. I wasn't out there to fill some romantic need. I was looking for a companion. Someone that I'd fall in love with. Everyone needs love, Tallulah."

I never knew. I always wondered how my beautiful, fun mother had remained single. I couldn't understand where all the men were. Why they weren't sending her flowers and asking her out. All along she'd been dating. "So the man who gave the sperm that created me didn't break you and destroy your belief in love after all?" Because that was what I had always thought.

My mom smiled softly. It was almost wistful. "No. He didn't. He taught me that life was hard. Not to trust easily and to be on guard. I was so young and naïve when I met him. Those were lessons I needed, and they were hard ones to learn. But I will always forever be thankful that with those lessons he left me with the most precious gift of my life. You."

She had told me many times in my life that my biological father gave her me so she could never hate him. But I hated him enough for both of us. Not because he didn't want me. But because I didn't understand how any man could not want her.

It's Time You Learned to Keep Living

CHAPTER 38

NASH

Haegan's funeral was in LA. My parents asked if I wanted to go. They'd fly out there with me. But I didn't. There was going to be media there, crying fans, people who never even knew him. It wasn't where I would say good-bye to him. Besides, I'd already done that as we'd been stuck in that car while they worked to get us out.

The local news covered the funeral. I didn't watch it. I couldn't. I was having nightmares that would wake me up in a cold sweat. Then I'd lie awake, staring at the ceiling for hours, afraid if I closed my eyes I'd see him there. See his lifeless body. Hear the crunching metal.

A week passed, and I hadn't gone back to school. I also

wouldn't accept visitors. Ryker was the only one who got in the house. But he was family. I couldn't keep him out. He talked a lot about shit at school, trying to get me to talk. To think about something else.

Tallulah had been on my mind a lot too. I'd texted her a million times, then deleted it before I sent it. I missed her almost as much as I hated her. I wanted to ask Ryker about her. About Mr. Dace. If he'd seen them together. But that would make him suspicious. He'd want to know why I was asking. I waited to see if he said anything about her. He didn't. Not once. He even told me about Blakely being suspended for being caught in the guys' restroom giving Hunter a blow job in one of the stalls. Hunter had also been suspended, and a freshman would be playing quarterback at the game Friday night. They would lose. They all knew it, and I could tell Ryker was pissed. Hunter wouldn't have it easy when he came back. The team would blame him for a long time over that loss.

When Ryker walked in my apartment over the garage at his normal time as he did every evening, he announced, "Brett Darby has been sitting outside with Tallulah at lunch."

The first he'd spoken of her. I didn't know how to react. I shrugged. I wanted to not care. But I did. Ryker dropped my classwork on the large leather ottoman in front of the sofa, where I was currently sitting, staring at the television but not watching it. ESPN was making their weekend predictions for college football scores. I never agreed with them anyway.

It wasn't Brett she wanted. It was fucking Coach D. Brett was stupid to think he could compete with a teacher. But then he didn't know that was his competition.

"Brett's got a scholarship to UCLA for tennis. A full fucking ride. He's popular. Girls like him," Ryker went on as if I didn't know any of this.

"How's the freshman doing at practice?" I asked, changing the subject to something I didn't give a shit about.

"We're gonna get our asses handed to us," he replied. "Heard he asked her out Friday night. After the game."

He wasn't letting it go. Damn his fucking meddling.

"Can't make a pass or what?" I asked as if he hadn't said anything about Tallulah.

"He's nervous. Got a lot riding on his back. He can't even remember the plays. It's a disaster."

"Work with him. Calm him down. Y'all might still pull this off. Our defense is the best in the state."

"Maybe. Wish Brady was in town. He'd be more help."

"Call him. See if he can give you some pointers. Maybe he can talk to the kid and help him out."

Ryker nodded. "Good idea. He's got a big game Saturday. I'll text him to give me a call when he has a chance."

"The freshman was undefeated in junior high school.

So it can't be he doesn't know how to play. He just needs work and confidence."

Ryker leaned forward and put his elbows on his knees. His gaze locked on me. The wrinkle between his brows meant he was about to say something I didn't want to hear. "You work with him."

"Fuck no," I replied immediately.

"Why? You feel so confident he can do it. That is what he needs to hear. You go work with him. Talk to him. Coach him. He needs someone that thinks he can do this. I personally don't."

"I wasn't a quarterback."

"Neither am I, but you sure thought I could do it," Ryker shot back at me.

I had been trying to change the subject off of Tallulah, and now I had this. What the fuck was I going to do now? "I'm not in the right frame of mind to help anyone."

Ryker continued to frown at me. "I get that this was hard on you. It won't ever go away. But it's been a week, and it's time you learned to keep living. Stop hiding out in this place. They're buried. Mrs. Wise had a heart attack, Nash. Haegan didn't kill her. She hit y'all when she had the heart attack. Her head fell forward and laid on the horn. They know all this now. No one blames you. There's no reason to stay here, locked away from life."

I knew that the people who had witnessed the wreck said it looked like Mrs. Wise had lost control. Maybe if Haegan hadn't been high, he'd have been able to react and get out of the way. But he'd not seen her car come barreling out of control, and she slammed into us head on. I hadn't seen it either. I had been looking in his direction. My mind wasn't clear. It might not have saved Mrs. Wise, but there was a chance Haegan would be alive.

"I'm coming back next week. I'll be there Monday." My dad had already said I had to get back to life. He'd let me stay out long enough.

"Come back tomorrow. Help me with this freshman."

"Not sure I can help him," I replied. That was the truth.

"It can't get any worse. At least we can say we tried. And it'll give you a distraction."

I stared at the television in front of me. This was all I had been doing for a week. I was tired of ESPN. But going back to school meant facing Tallulah. I already had to face the attention I was going to get from everyone else over the accident. Seeing her was going to make it harder.

"Okay," I agreed. I had to go ahead and get it over with. Dreading it made it worse.

Ryker grinned. "Really? You'll come back. Help me with Kip?"

"Who's Kip?"

"The freshman," he reminded me.

"Oh. Yeah."

He leaned back on the sofa and kicked his feet up on the ottoman. "You got beers hidden up here?"

I shook my head. "No. My parents are being strict with that shit. Mom is worried I have a drug problem."

He frowned. "And beer has something to do with that?

I shrugged. "In her eyes it's all the same."

"I don't need it anyway. I need to drink more water."

"I've got plenty of that in the fridge."

He turned his head and looked at me. "You ever gonna tell me what she did?"

We were back to Tallulah again.

"No," I said without pause.

He sighed. "Fine. But I think you're making a mistake."

I didn't argue. Because he'd push for the reason why again. I just let it go. I knew my reasons.

I Don't Smell Bad, Tallulah

CHAPTER 39

TALLULAH

Mr. Dace had been absent the day before when I'd arrived to his room to do my teacher's assistant work. He always left a note with instructions for me. I was thankful he wasn't there. Being in his class was hard enough. I could feel him watching me even when I wouldn't make eye contact with him. I'd almost told my mom about the kiss. But I hadn't because I was afraid of the outcome.

I wanted to forget it. Forget all he had said. Nash hadn't been back at school either, so I was living with the ache of losing him and not being sure why. After a week and not hearing from him, I had accepted that it was done. Between my broken heart and the secret I was hiding about Mr. Dace, I was a basket of emotions. I didn't want to leave my bedroom every day.

Brett Darby wasn't helping things. He wouldn't leave me alone. I just wanted some silence during lunch, but he thought my sitting alone meant I needed company. He had started showing up in the classes we didn't have together to walk me to my next one. He talked a lot. He liked to talk about himself. I knew he had been playing tennis since he was three, his favorite food was sushi, his middle name was Miller after his grandfather, he drank coffee every morning with three boiled eggs, and he wore a size-twelve shoe. I could promise you he didn't know any of that about me. He didn't require I talk. He did the talking, and as long as it appeared I was listening, he was happy.

That being the case, he had become harder to shake all week. My silence seemed to make him happy. In his head, I was enjoying his constant chatter. In reality, it was giving me an escape. At least when he was going on about his last tennis match or the next pair of shoes he was going to buy, I wasn't thinking about my problem with Mr. Dace or the pain left from Nash.

Yesterday Mr. Dace had asked in his note that I come in at seven fifteen to work on the grading log on his computer. I didn't like coming in early. There was hardly anyone there, and the teachers that were there were in their rooms working. No students were in the building. It was too quiet. If Mr. Dace wasn't going to be there, I would be fine. But the idea I'd be alone with him in his room made me nervous.

My hope that he would continue his absence when I was in his room was dashed as soon as I opened his door at exactly seven fifteen and saw him sitting at his desk. A sick knot I'd become all too familiar with tightened in my gut.

He smiled and waved to two cups of coffee on his desk along with some bakery items from the coffee shop down the road. I recognized the cups.

"Come have some caffeine and sugar. I'll get the computer set up for you. It's still in my bag. Just got here myself."

His tone was cheery and friendly. As if he hadn't told me he loved me and kissed me. He almost sounded normal. Like a teacher who wasn't hitting on his student. Maybe he was going to act like it never happened too.

"Okay, thanks," I replied, trying not to sound as nervous and uncomfortable as I was.

I took the cup of coffee but didn't take anything to eat and sat at the desk in front of him, ignoring the chair he had pulled up to his desk directly to the left of him. I wasn't sitting that close to him.

He looked over at me as he pulled his laptop out of his

bag and gave me a crooked grin. As if he was teasing me or thought I was being silly. "I don't smell bad, Tallulah," he said.

I was aware of that. He knew my reasons for sitting here. "This is a more comfortable spot. Gives us both plenty of room to work."

He opened his laptop, then walked around the table with it in his hands. I scooted back in my seat, trying to get more distance from him as he placed it on the desk in front of me. He didn't seem to notice I wanted my personal space. Or he didn't care.

"You know how this works." His voice had dropped lower. As if he were talking quietly so no one heard us. "The grades are in the basket on my desk."

I nodded, wishing he'd move away. Not continue to linger there in my personal space. It had moved past inappropriate now. I started to say something to him and ask him to move when he turned his head, and our faces were inches apart.

"I miss you," he said in a soft voice that made my spine tingle in a very bad way.

"Please move back," I said. My voice meant to be stern, but my building fear made it waver nervously.

"I won't hurt you, Tallulah. You know that." He leaned in like he was going to kiss me again, and I used my hands to shove him back. His chest was hard, and he didn't budge.

"You're thinking too much about this. No one will know. It's okay." He was whispering against my lips, and I jerked my head to the side to miss his mouth and it landed on my cheek.

He lingered there, and I closed my eyes as tears stung them. I hated this. I should have told my mother. I shouldn't have thought it was over. I made a huge mistake.

"I love you." His voice now sad. Much like it had been the last time. "He doesn't. He has not come back here. Another guy is moving in on you, and he's just letting him. I'd never shut you out. I'd always be here for you."

I fought back the scream building in my throat. If he'd move back, I could run. Run to get away from this. Run home and tell my mother. Stay in my room alone. I didn't want this attention. This had never been what I was after. Ever.

A sound from in the hallway came just when I needed it to. Mr. Dace was gone and back on his side of the desk in the blink of an eye. He'd moved fast. I didn't wait to see what the noise was. I was just thankful for it. Jumping up, I grabbed my book bag and headed for the door.

"Tallulah, don't go," he called out.

I didn't look back. But I did pause. "I'm not coming

back in here. You can tell the office whatever you want, but I am no longer your teacher's aide."

He sighed loudly. "I thought you were more mature than the other girls. But this is childish." His soft creepy voice had turned annoyed.

"Maybe because I'm seventeen," I replied, then opened the door. Freedom and safety were just in my reach. Stepping out of the room, I was so focused on getting free I didn't see them, but I heard her.

"There, Mr. Haswell," Pam said loudly.

I spun around to see Principal Haswell walking toward me with Pam right beside him, looking horrified. "I saw them. She was touching him. They were kissing."

Hearing her say the words, the way the accusation sounded, as if I was a part of what had just happened, sent my fear to a whole new level. What she was saying wasn't what happened.

"Why are you in Mr. Dace's room so early, Tallulah?" The authority in his tone did little to calm me. I was now close to terrified.

"I'm his teacher's aide. He asked me to come in early today." My voice cracked. My mouth felt too dry. I tried to swallow and couldn't.

"Is he in there?" Principal Haswell asked.

I nodded. "Yes, sir."

He walked past me and went directly to the door. With one twist of the knob he opened it and sent it swinging wide. I didn't go look. I was frozen in my spot. Pam stepped in front of me, and the smug look now on her face didn't surprise me.

"You deserve this, you little whore," she whispered.

I didn't know what to say. There was an explanation for what she saw, but I didn't owe it to her. I had to tell it to Mr. Haswell, though. I just didn't know if he would believe me. It was my word against both Mr. Dace's and Pam's.

"Why did you have a student in here with you alone at seven twenty in the morning?" Principal Haswell asked loudly.

"She's my aid. She was logging grades into the system."

Principal Haswell turned to look at me. "Is that what you were doing?" he asked me.

This was it. I had to make a choice. The truth or a lie.

*I Was Driving as If I
Were on the Defensive Line*

CHAPTER 40

NASH

Coming back today didn't mean I had to arrive on time. I was back even if it was thirty minutes after the late bell had rung. It wasn't that I hadn't gotten up early enough. It was that I had walked out to my Escalade about five times and turned around and come back inside. Every time I had gone out there and started to climb in the driver's seat, I'd fucking panicked.

I hadn't driven since the morning of the accident. Even when I was riding in the car with my parents, I had been gripping the door handle so tightly my knuckles turned white. I didn't like cars. The sounds, smells, and Haegan's lifeless face there beside me all came rushing back.

When I had finally gotten in the driver's seat this morning and cranked it up, my chest was so tight with anxiety I thought I was going to stop breathing. I'd fought through it, though. Forced my head to stop focusing on the wreck. After several deep breaths I had calmed down enough to drive. I drove slow. So damn slow. I'd never driven like this before in my life. Not even when I had been learning to drive.

But I was on guard. Every car around me, I mentally prepared myself for if they lost control or made a wrong move. I was driving as if I were on the defensive line. Ready to defend myself. Getting to school had taken much longer than necessary. But I had done it. I had driven. Alone. And I was alive.

It was one of those things you never really thought about. You took it for granted. Driving a car was what you looked forward to from the time you were a little kid. When you got to finally drive, you thought your parents' concern was stupid. You knew what you were doing You'd be fine. They needed to get over it. Nothing was going to happen to you. Until . . . it did. Then everything changed. For me, I'd never get in a car and causally drive, touch my phone, or take my eyes off the road. For Haegan, he'd never get that chance. It was over.

Sometimes lessons are learned the hard way. Other

times it isn't a lesson. It's a consequence. I had been spared. It had been a lesson for me. It seemed so fucking unfair that Haegan hadn't gotten that lesson. That his had been the end.

I walked into the school, and the hallway was quiet. That was expected with everyone in their first-period class. I didn't want to face the office, but I couldn't get into class without a tardy slip. The door, always propped open with a heavy cast-iron lion, had the breeze blowing through from the large box fan covered in dust. I walked inside, enjoying the cool breeze as a relief from the early morning heat outside. Mrs. Murphy was whispering with a concerned frown in the corner of the office with Mrs. Donna, the other secretary. They didn't notice me. I waited at the counter for someone to look my way, but whatever they were talking about seemed to have them both very upset.

I wasn't in a hurry to get to class anyway. I would get questions, more sympathy, and people would talk. I'd ignore it, but they would still be talking. It would be annoying. Just something I'd have to get over. At least I was alive to get over it. That was the one thought that kept coming back to me when I got annoyed or down the past week. Sure this was a shit situation. But I was alive. It could have been me.

"I just can't believe Dace. He's married. Has a baby

girl." Mrs. Murphy's whisper was a little too loud this time.
I strained to hear more. I didn't like Dace, but I didn't want
something to be wrong with his family. Although he sure
didn't act married. The man didn't even wear a ring.

"I'm glad they're not making her go in the same room as
him. She's a child," Mrs. Murphy continued. "It's a shame.
I am just horrified."

Mrs. Donna looked over then and saw me. She quickly
hushed Mrs. Murphy by pointing in my direction. Mrs.
Murphy's frown was still in place. "Oh, Nash, we are so
glad you're back. I've been praying for you. Are you doing
okay with it all?"

I could say a lot of things at that moment. About her
prayers and how I was doing. But instead I did what my
momma had raised me to do. Be polite. She didn't want
to know how I was really doing. She wanted to feel better about it all. She wanted her prayers to be working. So
tonight, when she went to bed, she'd feel better about the
tragedy and feel as if she did something to help.

"Thank you, ma'am," I replied. "I'm doing better."

She patted my hand. "Good. That was a terrible thing.
A terrible, terrible thing. It's never easy to lose a young life."

I nodded my head and kept my mouth shut. I would
much rather hear what Coach Dace had done. Anything to
get the attention off of me.

She signed a tardy slip and handed it to me. But when I tried to take it, she didn't let go. "You were dating Tallulah, weren't you? I know I saw y'all together."

In all my four years of high school Mrs. Murphy had never asked about my dating life. This was odd. "Uh, yes, ma'am," I replied. She'd also referred to me dating Tallulah in the past tense. Did that mean Tallulah was openly dating someone else? Was I going to be forced to watch her in the halls with another guy? Ryker had mentioned Brett, but damn that was fast.

She gave me an apologetic frown. "Well, she's had a hard morning. Might need a kind word when she returns to school."

"She's not here?" I asked, needing more information than that.

Mrs. Murphy's frown tightened. Then she chewed on her bottom lip. "She's here, but she won't be coming back to class. Might want to go check on her after school."

I wasn't happy with Tallulah. She'd fucking messed with my head. I thought I hated her. But I realized I didn't because at the moment all I could be was concerned. Worried. I needed more information. "What's wrong? Where is she?"

"You need to go on to class, Nash," Mrs. Donna said, stepping forward and touching Mrs. Murphy's arm. "Best it's not talked about."

Fuck that. She wasn't going to worry me, then tell me nothing. "Is she okay? Did she get hurt?"

Mrs. Murphy looked like she wanted to say more, but she looked at Mrs. Donna, who was shaking her head no with a stern expression. Dammit.

"Just go on to class," Mrs. Donna repeated.

"Why can't you tell me where she is?" I pushed.

Mrs. Murphy opened her mouth to say something more when her eyes went to the door behind me.

"I'm Charlotte Dace. Where is my husband?" the woman demanded.

Mrs. Murphy walked around the counter. "Right this way," she told her.

Charlotte Dace was tall, thin, blond, had larger lips than was normal, and walked like someone who was in one of those beauty pageants. She followed behind Mrs. Murphy. I watched them go until the door to the principal's office opened.

Coach D stepped forward, and his eyes locked on his wife's. They were scared. He was scared. "You sorry piece of shit!" she screamed.

"Oh my," Mrs. Donna whispered.

The door closed behind them as Charlotte Dace slammed it shut.

Mrs. Murphy turned to look at me, and her eyes were round with anxiety.

I didn't need an explanation anymore. I understood what was going on.

Tallulah and Coach Dickhead had been caught.

Men like Him, They Don't Get Better

CHAPTER 41

TALLULAH

I heard her scream. I was numb now, though. I'd faced it. Taken the hard road instead of the easy. It would have been much less complicated to lie. Ignore it. But I couldn't lie. Not anymore. I was scared of him. It was time I dealt with all the repercussions and told the truth, before he took it too far.

My mother's hand squeezed mine as she held it tightly. The police officer called in was Officer Mike. I'd known him since I was a kid. He was Santa in the town square during the holidays. He gave out candy at the station on Halloween dressed as Superman. He was the one who always did the safety seminars in the school auditorium.

Everyone knew Officer Mike. When he had walked in the counselor's office where my mother and I waited, I had been relieved. Somewhat comforted.

"I've had some records pulled on Dace, and it appears this isn't the first time. He left the last school after whispers began to circulate that he was having relations with one of his students. However, her parents never filed a complaint, and she never came forward." He paused and lifted his gaze from the file in front of him. "It's a brave thing to do, Tallulah."

I didn't feel very brave at the moment. I was sick with fear. I didn't know what would happen next. If I was going to be expected to speak to a judge, or go to court, or face Mr. Dace again. I didn't want to. Not now.

"Why didn't the school check into that before hiring him?" My mother was upset. She was fighting back tears, and I knew controlling her emotions was difficult for her.

Officer Mike shrugged. "I don't know. I will say it took some digging. With no actual complaint filed, it wasn't easily accessible. But I knew the right people to call to find out."

Mother pressed her fingers to her temple and closed her eyes. "His wife," she said with a tight voice. "What she must feel." She opened her eyes again. "You said they had a child. How old is she?"

"Three."

"Jesus," my mother muttered. "He's a sick man, and he has a daughter. How would he feel if this happened with his daughter one day? Tallulah's just a child herself."

Officer Mike gave a slow nod. "Yes. But men like Dace see a woman."

Mom shot up from her seat and began to pace the room. "She's seventeen. He is ten years older than her. She's naïve. She's sweet and kind. She worries about her grades."

All of this really had no relevance, but to my mother it did.

"I've got everything, Tallulah?" Officer Mike asked me. "This is it? All of it, or were there any other incidents you need to tell me about?"

I shook my head. "Just those two. The other times he had been friendly. Maybe too friendly, but he had never done anything. Not until last week."

Officer Mike stood. "I'll make sure he doesn't step foot in a school system again."

"Good!" my mother said, her eyes filling with tears again.

With that, Officer Mike left the room.

Mrs. Milly, the school counselor, stepped back inside. She looked from me to my mom. Then she stuck her glasses that were perched on her head back on her nose. "You're free to go now. I'm suggesting that Tallulah take a day to settle her nerves before returning to classes."

My mother nodded. "Yes. She will. Thank you."

Mrs. Milly turned to look at me. "I had been watching him. I'd seen his gaze going where it shouldn't. I know coming forward with this was hard. But it was for the best. Men like him, they don't get better."

I didn't know how to respond to that. Too much had happened. My head hurt. My chest ached, and I never wanted to walk back into this school again. Because I knew that although the adults believed me . . . not all the students would.

My mother took my arm and held it tightly, as if I needed her strength to walk. I wasn't falling apart. She might be, but I was just scared of all the things I would face now. I hadn't been damaged. I hadn't actually been frightened until this morning. Mr. Dace had pushed too hard. The kiss had just startled me, made me uncomfortable. But today he'd seemed more unstable.

I walked with my mother into the hallway. She was quiet, and so was I. From the moment I told Principal Haswell, "Mr. Dace has been making advances to me. Once before, a week ago, and today. I didn't want it, and I told him to stop," everything changed.

Pam had been sent to the office to wait to speak to the

counselor before going to class. I had been taken to the assistant principal's office, while Mr. Dace had been taken to Principal Haswell's office.

My mother had arrived first. Principal Haswell had called her. Then Officer Mike. I didn't know what Mr. Dace was claiming. I knew he wasn't telling the truth. It was going to be my word against his and possibly Pam's. She was the only witness. I already knew she wasn't going to side with me. She wanted me to have been in the wrong. The girls who loved him wouldn't want to believe he was wrong. The guys on the football team would be angry that I was accusing their coach of something that could have him fired.

I knew all this when I told the truth. But I wasn't going to lie.

I scanned the hallway to see if anyone was out here. I didn't want to face a student before I left. The rumors would be bad enough already. My gaze landed on the one person I wasn't expecting. The one I didn't want to see, yet I couldn't stop thinking about. The guy who had crushed me and would now hate me. Nash.

He stood there silently in the hallway. His backpack over his shoulder. The Lawton Lions duffel bag he'd carried when he played football in his left hand. That was odd. Why would he be carrying his football gear around?

I lifted my eyes back to meet his, and there was disgust there. Even hate. It felt ice cold and painful as it sank in that he knew, and he didn't believe the best. He assumed the worst. I had hoped of all students he'd be the one to believe in me. To know I'd never do what I was going to be accused of. But even Nash thought I could do it. If he didn't believe me, no one would.

How would I come back here and face this? Being made fun of because I was fat hadn't been easy, but I could accept it. Live through it. But being accused of something like this . . . I just didn't know if I could.

"Ignore that," Mother whispered beside me.

If only I could. If only I didn't care. If only I didn't love him.

*I Was Tired of Being
the Center of Attention*

CHAPTER 42

NASH

Ryker met me outside my first period. I'd heard her name whispered in class, but no one had said anything. We'd been working on a paper due next week. It was supposed to be silent, but I had no doubt one of the many whispering and looking my way would have told me about Tallulah and Dace.

"Wishing I hadn't pushed for you to come back today," he said.

I shrugged. "Not my problem. Though I feel bad for his wife and kid."

Ryker's eyes went wide. "He's married with a kid?"

I nodded. I wouldn't have told anyone else that. But

Ryker was different. He might as well have been my brother. He also didn't talk shit about people.

"Damn," he muttered.

"I brought my practice shit. I'll be ready to help after school. Make sure that quarterback is ready."

Ryker smiled then. "I will."

Having something to do with football helped me not keep thinking about Tallulah. "What time . . ." I began to ask what time he wanted to get started when I saw her locker. I paused. My stomach turned like I'd eaten something bad.

In red lipstick the word *SLUT* was written horizontally and in large letters covering the entire front of Tallulah's locker. I stared at it, unable to take another step. My head was telling me she deserved it, but the sickness in my stomach didn't agree. No one deserved that. It was cruel and vicious. Yes, she'd made a fucking mistake. There was a good chance she didn't know he was married and had a kid. Hell, I didn't know. Ryker didn't know. Dace didn't advertise it.

He was still a teacher, and she'd been dating me. At least I thought we had something. I had been her cover. What I was feeling wasn't hate. It was disappointment and heartache. I'd thought she was different. Special. But she wasn't. Truth was, most of the girls in this school would have fallen for him if he'd given them the chance. He was the "hot teacher," and he had gone after Tallulah. That didn't make her a monster. It made her normal. Average. The same.

"I'll help you clean it," Ryker said.

I hadn't needed to say anything to him. He knew this was hard on me. But he wasn't going to let something like that slide by, either. "I doubt she knew he was married. He was older, smarter, and could easily manipulate a teenage girl. I'm not making excuses for her. I just thought I'd point out I don't think Tallulah should be the one at fault here."

She'd done it. She'd hurt me. I could fault her for that. "I'll go see what the janitor has to get that off," I replied. I'd keep my thoughts to myself. They made me vulnerable. I didn't want that. No one needed to know how badly she'd hurt me.

"I'll go get us an excuse for class," Ryker said, then headed the other way.

I started toward the janitor's room when Pam walked in front of me. "It was me who caught them," she announced smugly. As if she'd won an award.

"Lucky you," I drawled, and kept walking.

"She wasn't good enough for you anyway. She's a slut. Who sleeps with a teacher, anyway?"

I paused. Her words pissed me off. I didn't want to think too deeply about why, but I knew it was because she

was making accusations she had no proof of. I knew Tallulah
well enough to know she wasn't having sex with the man.

"Really? You caught them going at it?" I asked sarcasti-
cally.

She shifted her feet and tilted her chin back as if she was
important. "No, but I saw them touching. Kissing." She
said the last part as if it was all the proof we needed.

"Last time I checked, you were well aware of the vast
difference between kissing and sex, Pam. I wasn't aware
kissing made someone a slut. If so, then this entire school is
full of them. Me included."

She rolled her eyes. "That's not what I meant. The rest
of the school wasn't kissing a married man and a teacher!"

I took a step toward her, my glare locked on her. "Did
you know he was married?" I asked, already knowing the
answer.

She shrugged. "I didn't ask."

"Did you look at his hand? Was he wearing a wedding
band?"

Her shrug this time was smaller, with less conviction.
"He was still a teacher."

I laughed then. The empty kind I was so fucking good
at. "A teacher you threw yourself at every chance you
got. But you weren't the only one who thought he was
hot. I heard it daily." I waved my hand toward the packed

hallway. I noticed we had drawn a crowd. "I bet you'd be hard pressed to find one girl in this high school who didn't have a crush on Mr. Dace. Yet he wanted Tallulah, so that makes her a slut. He was the adult. He knew better."

As my voice got louder and I defended Tallulah not only to Pam but the others listening, I accepted that what I was saying was true. I didn't forgive her. Because it had been me she'd hurt. But I didn't think it made her a slut. I thought it made her naïve and stupid.

Pam threw her hands up dramatically. "Whatever. Take up for her. She caused us to lose a great teacher and football coach. Not that you care about football anymore." She snarled the last bit, wanting to hurt me. Embarrass me. It didn't work.

"No one wants to hear your shit, Pam. Go on," Asa said, stepping up beside me. "Besides, Coach D wasn't that great of a coach. The team will be fine without him. And as for literature, I was failing his class. He sucked as a teacher."

Asa struggled to pay attention in most classes. He thought all teachers sucked. But I was grateful for his stepping in. Not because I couldn't handle Pam, but because I was tired of being the center of attention.

Pam swung her long hair over her shoulder and stalked away. She was done arguing. Thank God.

"You're welcome," Asa said, grinning.

"Thanks, I gotta go."

"Where you going? Second period is the other way."

"Janitor's closet. I need to clean her locker." I didn't say whose. I didn't have to. There was only one locker that needed cleaning in this school.

"I'll go with you."

"It's okay. Ryker's getting us excuses and helping me."

Asa nodded. "Okay. If you don't need me, I'll see you after class."

"We got it. But thanks."

I began walking again when Asa called out. "For the record, I think we don't know the real story. I don't think she did it."

If I hadn't witnessed the kiss myself, I probably wouldn't have believed it either. I didn't respond because I had nothing to say. My secret would remain just that. Especially now.

CHAPTER 43

TALLULAH

All weekend, no one called. You can know you don't have friends. But it's never more obvious than when something bad happens. There's no one to call you. No one to stop by to check on you. No one to believe you.

I already knew I was friendless. I should have grown used to it. But the past few weeks I hadn't felt lonely. I'd had Nash. He was my friend. He made me feel a part of something. Like I fit in. Like this world cared if I was alive or dead. Like I was important too.

That had been fleeting. Gone too soon. I wished for the millionth time I hadn't known what it felt like. Love, friendship, acceptance. Before I'd been clueless. It had been easier then. My books had been enough.

Nash had changed it all for me. I would have to learn to make it through alone again. Every day at school with no one speaking to me. They'd whisper and point again. Didn't matter what size I was. Being thin didn't save me from being an outcast. When I had walked all summer and used my drive for revenge to keep me going, I had honestly believed that being thin would solve all my problems. How stupid was that?

I hadn't fit in then, and I didn't now. I never would. I wish I hadn't even tried. If I had stayed overweight, then Mr. Dace would have never noticed me. He'd never have kissed me. The school wouldn't hate me.

Sitting in my car, I watched as others began to arrive at school. They all were excited to be here. They had groups. Friends waiting on them. And they'd all see me and blame me. I'd be the outcast. I imagined that was worse than being invisible. If only I could just be invisible again.

I waited. Watched. And gave myself pep talks that did little good. I hadn't heard anything all weekend about what Mr. Dace was going to do. If he was going to deny it and take this to court to clear his name, which I found could be a possibility. I knew he wouldn't be here, though. My mother had made sure I wasn't going to face him again at school.

I'd almost turned around and gone back inside the house to beg her to let me homeschool. But I knew she would let me. She would want to protect me. She wouldn't make me face this. I had to face it. I had to stand up for myself. If I didn't come back, they would all think I was guilty. That I had been a willing participant.

Stepping out of the car, I felt my hands tremble. I fisted them tightly at my sides. I wasn't going to be that weak. I could do this. I had done nothing wrong.

I straightened my shoulders. Took my backpack and put it over my shoulder, then headed for the doors. I didn't make eye contact with those still lingering outside. I kept walking. Held my head high. I had nothing to be ashamed of.

They were looking. I could feel them. It was like time stood still, and they all turned their attention to me. My face heated. My heart raced. I kept moving forward. They couldn't hurt me.

"SLUT!" someone yelled out. I had prepared myself for that. It was so far from the truth it was almost funny. Almost.

I didn't turn to see which girl had thought it was acceptable to yell slut at someone else. I didn't care. I continued to remind myself that I knew the truth. That was all that mattered. I knew.

With a jerk of the door, I opened it and went inside. More people. More eyes. More conversations paused as they spotted me. I didn't stop. I kept moving.

"No one wants you here, slut," one said as I passed by.

"Go home, you whore," another called out.

"Liar!" someone else called out.

I did the only thing I could. I ignored it all.

Until a guy I didn't know, who had to be younger than me, stepped in my path and grinned. "I'll fuck you on a desk if you want? Or are you just into older men?"

Laughter erupted around him.

I went to move around him, and he shifted to block me once more. I glared up at him this time. "Get out of my way," I said firmly.

"Aww, don't be like that, baby. I just want a taste of what had Coach D pulling down his pants in the classroom."

I should have expected this. Rumors to grow into ridiculous lies. I went to move around him again. Once more, he made sure I couldn't.

"You don't want her STDs," a female voice called out. I'd heard that voice before, but I didn't look to see who it was.

The guy smirked. "She doesn't seem that easy to me. I think she only gives it to the older guys."

"That's enough, dipshit," Nash said angrily, and I turned my head this time to see him making his way through the crowd toward me.

The guy's demeanor changed. "Sorry, man. Just having some fun with the school teacher banger."

Nash was in his face then. He shoved him back hard with his good arm. "Fuck off," he ordered.

The kid swallowed hard and his Adam's apple bobbed, then he turned and hurried down the hall. Nash look around. "Jesus, move on. Get a life," he yelled.

People began to move away. It was like magic. They all turned and began talking again. I was no longer the entertainment. All because of Nash. He had come to my rescue. He cared.

"Thank you," I said in shock that of all people it had been Nash to stand up for me. He didn't look at me right away. His back was still to me. His shoulders tense. When he did finally move, my heart leaped. He was going to talk to me.

His eyes were void of emotion. He didn't smile or seem concerned. Nothing. He didn't give me long to figure out what that meant. "This means nothing. Don't read into it. I'm a nice guy. I don't allow bullying when I see it. That's all this was."

His words still lingered, crushing my soul and my

hopes as he walked away. I didn't watch him go. It took all my attention to keep from falling apart. For a moment I had let my guard down. And that easily I was broken yet again. When I could manage to move one foot in front of the other, I walked to my locker.

I wouldn't do it again. I wouldn't let myself believe in love. Or even in something as simple as a friend. Those things weren't mine to have.

Getting the things I would need from my locker was mindless. I didn't have to think to do it. I needed a distraction. Something to ease Nash's words as they played over and over in my head.

"Whore," Pam hissed as she walked up to my locker. "I saw you. You're a whore. You deserve all of this."

She didn't stick around to continue. She'd said what she needed, so she hurried away. Pam was evil, yet she had friends. People who she could talk to. She was never alone. She'd never been the outcast. Why she thrived on seeing me alone and hated, I didn't know. I'd done nothing to her. I'd done nothing to anyone. Until a few weeks ago most of them hadn't realized I existed. Yet we'd gone to school together our entire lives.

I didn't understand that kind of cruelty. I never wished this on anyone. Not even Pam.

I Could Be a Lion Again
CHAPTER 44

NASH

I'd worked out with the team today. After standing on the side of the field Friday night and watching the freshman throw a winning touchdown, I had decided I could be a part of this. I'd helped with that. His confidence had been built, and although he wouldn't be first string until his junior year, he was ready when Hunter wasn't.

I watched them practice for an hour. Standing there smelling the grass and feeling the heat from the sun felt good. It was like going home. This was and would always be a part of me. I'd grown up loving this game. I always would. Even if my years of playing it were over. That didn't mean I was losing the field all together.

"I've got physical therapy," I called out to Ryker. "I gotta go."

He nodded, and the smile on his face from just having me down here made me feel a part of something again.

"Nash, wait," Coach Rich called out.

I paused and waited as he jogged over to me. He seemed happy to see me. At least I thought he was. But I was suddenly worried he was about to tell me not to come to practice. Because I wasn't on this team anymore. Normally he didn't let others watch. Much less stand on the field.

"What you did with Kip was amazing. I'd already prepared myself for a disaster Friday night. But Ryker and Kip said you came and helped him."

I shrugged. "He just needed a confidence boost. I watched his games from last year. He's good. A more natural talent than Hunter in my opinion."

Coach grinned. "I saw that Friday night. It got me thinking. This . . ." He sighed and ran a hand through his hair. "This shit with Dace. He's gone. He won't be coming back. Even if she did pursue him. He caved. He's gone. And they're not going to be able to replace a defense coordinator slash literature teacher with one paycheck overnight. I need help. I can handle things, but it would be easier and more successful if I had someone who the guys had a relationship with watching them and making suggestions. I'd like you to step in and be a part of the team again. It's not a paid job of course. They can't hire a kid. But I could use you. This team could."

He was asking me to coach? Me? I stood there, staring at him in shock. When he'd started talking about Dace, I'd gotten nauseated and wanted to get away. Forget that shit. But he'd blindsided me. With a chance to be down here. I could be a Lion again.

"Seriously?" I asked. Because if this was a joke, I needed to know now.

He nodded. "Completely."

"Yes" was all that I could get to come out of my mouth. I was speechless otherwise.

He slapped me on the back. "Welcome back, son."

I nodded. I couldn't even say thank you. My eyes locked on Ryker, who was watching us. He saluted me with a smile that said he knew what had just happened. "Thanks, Coach Rich," I finally said.

"Don't thank me. Just win us some games."

Those words didn't scare me. My dad had been telling me that all my life. I worked good under pressure.

Coach Rich walked back to the others, and I headed for the parking lot. I'd have to adjust my physical therapy schedule. Because my afternoons were about to be busy once again.

Smiling, I was lost in the first trace of happiness I'd felt since the accident. My smile slowly weakened as I thought of Haegan. Then, as if fate liked to kick me in the ass, I saw Tallulah. She was walking to her car. Her arms full of books and her backpack full. She looked miserable. I knew the entire school had talked about her today. Made jokes at her expense. Blamed her for Dace being gone.

But I couldn't fight all her battles. I couldn't shut them all up. She'd asked for this. I had nothing to do with it. I'd been hurt in the crossfire. But if I caught anyone else in her face, taunting her, I'd step in. I already knew that without having to think about it.

Right now I wanted to go lighten her load and help her with her books. Which fucking sucked ass because I shouldn't want to be near her. I shouldn't care what others said. She had kissed a teacher. The fact he was married made it worse, but I had decided she hadn't known that. She'd never have done it if she'd known. He'd been after her since the first day of school. I'd seen it. She hadn't flirted with him. She hadn't tried to get his attention.

What she had done was return his attraction and respond to his advances. I stood there watching as she dropped a few books and sighed wearily, then bent down to put the other books on the ground. She began to stack them up again. The pile was too tall for her to carry. She stood up and looked down at it, then at her car.

Why was she carrying so many books home anyway? No one had that much homework. I fought back going to help her. I didn't need to be near her. Being so close I could smell her, seeing her eyes so full of hope for forgiveness today had about been my undoing. I didn't want to stay away from her. Even with all she had done I missed her.

She bent down and picked up half the stack, then carried it to her car. I was so focused on her I didn't notice Brett pick up the other books she'd left behind. He was coming up behind her when I noticed him. She turned and jumped, startled to see him, then she smiled. That sweet smile that did things to me.

They talked. She tried to take the books, but he put them in her car for her. Then they talked some more. I needed to get in my fucking Escalade and go to physical therapy. But then they'd see me. She'd see me. She'd see me seeing them. Shit. That was too damn convoluted. I was making too much out of this. We were over. Right? I was done. Then I had to stop acting like I had to hide from her.

I picked my duffel up and headed to my Escalade. I knew she saw me when the hairs on my arms stood up and I got a tingle down my spine. My body even reacted to her when I wasn't looking. It was like it knew she was there, and it went on high alert. Damn traitor.

I cracked and shifted my gaze in her direction. She was

watching me. I held her gaze for a moment. It was wrong. I shouldn't. If I was done and this was over, I had to act like it. Not lock gazes with her when she's talking to another guy. That said shit. Shit I wasn't going to follow through with. Because I didn't trust her. I never would again.

It was Tallulah who broke the stare. She shifted her attention back to Brent. Her smile was tighter now. Less real. Less soft. More forced. But he wouldn't know that. He didn't know her like I did. I climbed in my Escalade, telling myself this was for the best. It was the only way to protect my head and heart. But damn if it didn't hurt like hell.

Like a Wolf about to Protect Its Young
CHAPTER 45

TALLULAH

After lunch and the constant verbal lashing I was taking from the rest of the student body, I went to the counselor to discuss the possibility of me homeschooling for the rest of the semester. I knew there was a program where you could homeschool but remain on the same curriculum as the school. It was run by the county. I needed all the information on it before I took it to my mother. She'd have questions.

I was a distraction in class. Twice before lunch teachers had been forced to stop class and talk to everyone about not spreading rumors. It was all because they were whispering about me, throwing paper at the back of my head, and laughing at each other's jokes centered on me. I couldn't learn in that environment, and neither could anyone else. The teachers' frustration was obvious. I should have known I couldn't come back here. Thinking I could deal with this and it would be okay was crazy.

The counselor called my mother, and we discussed it in her office over speakerphone. When it was over, I was sent to each teacher's class to get all the work I needed for the next two weeks so I wouldn't get behind while we were switching me over to the virtual school system. It had been successful in other schools in the county. But no one at Lawton had tried it yet.

When school ended, I then had to meet the counselor in the library to get the paperwork and instructions for my mom to get me registered. We went over how to handle it if I chose to return. It was a lot of information, but it kept my mind off the reason I was doing this.

As I was leaving, Mrs. Milly said she hoped in time I'd come back. She would miss my smiling face in the hallway. That was the first time I teared up. Until she said that I had assumed my absence would go unnoticed. Or simply that no one would care. Hearing her say it, even if she was the counselor, made me feel wanted. Just a little.

I sat outside my house now. My car full of books that Brett had helped me load after I dropped them three times in my attempt to carry them. Brett had also told me he would miss me. He hoped I would come back. Then he'd asked for my phone number and if he could text me. Or even call sometime. I had said yes, and at that moment Nash had locked eyes with me.

He wouldn't miss me. My absence would be a relief to him.

This morning I had thought no one cared. But now I knew two people did. Yes, I was counting Mrs. Milly. When you're as limited on friends as I was, you counted it all. Even the adults paid to care.

Being the biggest slut at Lawton High and never having had sex was ironic. I'd thought about that a lot today too. At first it had seemed unfair, but I had moved past that. Life wasn't fair. Haegan's family would agree with me. This was bad, but it could be worse. My momma had always reminded me that when I had a bad day, there was someone out there who would trade places with me. Never to get down, but be thankful for what I did have.

I was trying to do that, but it was hard. Especially when your car was loaded down with books you wouldn't normally need yet, but they'd be a part of this semester's reading. Then the textbooks that couldn't be replaced online. I had to bring those, too.

The front door opened, and Momma came walking out.

She had been watching for me, and I hadn't gotten out of my car fast enough for her. The smile on her face wasn't real. She was worried about me and trying to cheer me up. I was betting there was chocolate pound cake and ice cream waiting on me inside. That was her cure-all.

I opened my car door and got out of the car. "I'm coming," I assured her.

"Thought you might need help carrying things," she said, her voice light with false jolliness.

"Momma, today was bad. You already know this. Acting happy won't cheer me up. This sucks. All of it. I will get over it, though. So stop forcing your smile. It looks painful."

Her smile dropped, and she rung her hands in front of her. "Oh, honey, I've been worried sick all day."

I didn't sugarcoat it. She knew the truth. She'd talked to the counselor. "They liked Mr. Dace. They don't want to think he did anything wrong. So it has to be my fault. I can't change their minds. And I can't go to school with them. They don't want me there, and I no longer want to be there."

Her eyes filled with tears. "I'd thought this year would be your best. You'd go to prom, and go on dates. You'd have friends and go to football games. You would love going to school every morning. All the things you missed. And that . . . that . . . bastard took that from you."

She looked so distraught I wanted to reassure her, but what could I say? Promise that I'd get to do those things? It was my senior year. This was it. I wouldn't do any of it. I wouldn't even go to school.

"Let's go inside and eat the pound cake and ice cream I know is in there," I suggested.

She nodded and sniffled. "Okay. I made fudge topping, too. For the ice cream," she told me.

I'd have to walk extra miles tomorrow, but then I would have more time. Working from home would make things go quicker. I'd have more time for my walks. And for reading. Tonight I'd enjoy the sugar and feel bad for myself. Tomorrow I'd get over it. Move on. Figure out my new schedule.

We started to walk inside the house when an older model silver BMW that needed to be washed badly pulled into the driveway. Both of us turned to look at who it was. We didn't get visitors often. The blond hair was the first thing I saw. She had a lot of it. And she was tall. Striking, even. I'd never seen her in my life.

"Can I help you?" my mother asked, smiling in her friendly way.

"Yes." She looked from my mother to me. "I'm here to speak with you and your daughter." She walked toward us and held out her hand. "I'm Charlotte Dace."

And just like that my sweet momma's smile fell, and a look of ferocity came over her face. Much like a wolf about to protect its young. I almost expected her to snarl and show her teeth next. "Then you should have had your lawyer contact ours," Mother told her in a firm voice that meant business. She also took that moment to step in front of me as if she needed to protect me from Charlotte Dace.

Charlotte didn't seem to get upset or prepare to attack her. She remained calm. "I can understand your reaction. If she were my daughter, I'd feel the same way. However, we don't need a lawyer. There is no point in it. I had been prepared to stand beside my husband and defend him. I called a lawyer and set up an appointment. I was determined he'd been seduced by a Lolita.

"But he didn't let me go much further. He admitted it all. He said she had fought off his advances both times. She was naïve and young. Innocent and had no idea how to deal with attention from a grown man. That attracted him more. Then, when I wanted to believe this was a one-time instance, he admitted to two other underage girls he'd had affairs with. Girls who had been willing. And each time he said he loved them."

She stopped then.

I stood silently. I knew this already—well I knew about

one other girl. The one Officer Mike had mentioned.

"Would you like to come inside?" Mom asked, her ferocious demeanor now extinguished.

Charlotte nodded. "Yes, please. I'd like to ask Tallulah a few things, if that's okay with you. I need closure on this. I'm filing for divorce, but I have a long road ahead of me. I intend to fight for full custody of our daughter."

"I don't blame you," Mom replied. Then she looked at me. "Are you okay with talking to her?"

I was. "Yes," I told her.

"Thank you," Charlotte said. "I know this hasn't been easy for you. I don't want to upset you any more than you've already been. I'd just like to ask you a few things to see how much of the truth he's given me."

I could understand that. "Okay."

We went inside, and the smell of my mother's pound cake filled the air. It was the first comfort I'd felt all day. It meant I was home. The insecurity that had settled over me when Charlotte Dace introduced herself was gone.

"Please have a seat," Mother said, motioning toward the sofa. "Can I get you coffee? Some pound cake?"

Charlotte shook her head. "No thank you. I won't take much of your time. I appreciate this."

Mom sat down beside me on the love seat. Her hand rested on my knee. It was her show of support.

Charlotte shifted in her seat and crossed her legs. "When did he tell you he loved you?"

"A little over a week ago. He kissed me, and I ran out of the room and into the nearest restroom. He followed me inside. Told me there."

She nodded. "Did he tell you he was married?"

I shook my head. "No. I had no idea. But then it wouldn't have mattered because I didn't want his attention."

"Do you think he's done this with any other girls at the school?"

I thought for a moment, then shook my head. "No . . . I didn't pay attention to him unless I was in his class. I never once thought of him as more than a teacher."

She looked up at the photo of me from two years ago that sat on the mantel. "You've lost weight," she said.

"Yes."

She moved her gaze back to me. "When? I mean, if you don't mind me asking."

"This summer," I told her.

She sighed. "He said you were different from the others. You didn't flirt and had no idea how beautiful you were. He said you were smart and mature for your age. I see now why you're so different." She didn't mean it in a bad way; she was just speaking her thoughts.

She stood up. "I believe my husband is unstable. Mentally he has some sickness. It's the young girls. He is drawn to them. If he contacts you, I'd call the police. I don't know him. I realize I'm living with a man that I don't know at all, and I'm terrified."

My mother stood up too. "I'm sorry for you and your daughter," she said.

Charlotte nodded. "I'm sorry for the harm he's done here, too."

Mom walked Charlotte to the door, and I watched them go. Relieved there would be no court. That I wouldn't have to defend myself but worried about the little girl who wouldn't have a father. I'd never had one. But she'd known what it felt like to have a dad, and she was going to lose that. I imagined that would be harder.

That Girl Ain't Got a Selfish,
Mean Bone in Her Body

CHAPTER 46

NASH

I'd be lying if I said I wasn't looking for her. Because I was. I had been since I walked out of first period. Her car hadn't been in her parking spot when I got here this morning, and I had been late. Tallulah was never late. It was normal for me to wonder where she was. I was just curious.

Fuck that. I was worried. She'd had a hard day yesterday. I hadn't talked to her, but I had heard enough to know things had been hell for her. Now she was nowhere, and I was ready to leave school and go check on her. But that wasn't my place.

Instead of leaving, I began scanning the crowd in the hallway for Brett. He should know. He'd been up her ass since things had ended with us. And after what I saw yesterday, he didn't give a shit about the Dace stuff. It hadn't affected him like it affected me, though. She wasn't dating him and messing around with Dace at the same time.

I looked for him. It wasn't until I'd thought of every scenario my imagination could come up with through second and third period that I found Brett at his locker on my way to lunch. I didn't know the guy well. I knew of him. He'd been to a couple field parties. But we weren't what you considered friends. Merely acquaintances.

"Hey," I said, stopping beside his locker before I could talk myself out of it. If I didn't find out, it was going to drive me fucking nuts.

He turned, and his body instantly tensed when he saw me. "Nash."

He knew my name. That was good. "Yeah. I saw you talking to Tallulah yesterday. Do you know where she is today?"

He studied me a moment. The uncertainty on his face. For a moment I thought he may tell me to go fuck myself. But finally he nodded. "Yeah. I know."

Nothing more. He didn't elaborate, give me any more information. He was going to make me ask for it. Fine. I'd ask. "Then where is she?" The annoyance in my tone was obvious.

He lifted a shoulder, then closed his locker door. "If you don't know, then she must not have wanted you to. Besides, she said y'all were done. You ended it."

I had ended it, but she'd kissed the motherfucking teacher. I had never liked tennis. I really didn't like it at this moment. "I had my reasons. Now, where is she?" I demanded this time, instead of asking.

He did that stupid quiet-stare thing again. My patience was thinning. "And I guess your reason was the Mr. Dace stuff?" He started to walk away from me then. Just like that, he thought he could just walk off. He acted like my being upset that she was kissing a teacher was stupid. Like I should overlook it.

"I guess you'd forgive her, then," I blurted out. "Overlook the fact she was using you? She was having an affair with a teacher the whole time?"

Brett stopped. He turned back to me. "If you believe what you're saying, then you do not deserve her. The girl I've spent less than ten hours talking to, she'd never do what she's being accused of."

I wanted to tell him that I had seen it. I knew the fucking truth before anyone else. But I didn't. That would make this harder on her. I wasn't going to hurt her any more than she was already hurt. She'd brought it on herself, but that didn't mean I would make it worse.

He walked off then, and I let him. He wasn't going to give me answers. He was the one kid in the school who believed her. Did she feel guilty about that? Or was she trying to manipulate him? Even as I thought it, I knew it didn't fit. Tallulah wasn't like that. This whole situation didn't make sense. The girl I knew. The girl Brett thought he knew . . . she didn't do this.

"Homeschool." Ryker said that one word as he walked up beside me. "She couldn't take it yesterday. She opted out. She's homeschooling."

My stomach dropped. Tallulah wasn't here. She was at home. She was going to stay at home. Away from it all. Safe. Because they'd been too hard on her. She'd taken too much. They'd finally given her more than she could take.

I stood there in the hallway, oblivious to the people walking by and what they were saying. All I could think was I'd never see her again. She'd stay tucked away. Her smile wouldn't light up the hallway. Her laugh was gone.

Was that what she deserved? Had her kissing a teacher really been that bad? Why did they hate her so damn much for it? I had a reason, but no one else did. Yet they'd cracked her. Where years of making fat jokes and laughing at her hadn't sent her home, this had.

Could there be another explanation? I didn't see how there could. I'd seen them kiss. Pam had seen them kiss.

Dace was fired. What other explanation was there? How was she innocent? I wanted her to be. God, I wanted her to be. But she couldn't be. Could she? Was there a scenario I was missing?

"It's for the best," Ryker said as his hand rested on my shoulder. "They were never going to let it go. She'd have dealt with it the rest of the year. Pam and her bunch didn't like Tallulah walking into school looking better than they ever had. She took attention off them. They were jealous. Pam has this ammunition, and she will not let it die. It's better for Tallulah to homeschool."

"She'd never given up before. They'd never pushed her to run. Tallulah doesn't run."

Ryker shrugged. "This was different. She was being accused of sleeping with a teacher, one who is married. Some think she's lying on him. Some think she seduced him. But both sides blame her."

That fucking annoyed me. "He was the adult," I said angrily.

Ryker shrugged. "Yeah. But they still blame her."

"It's not fair." It wasn't. They were all so damn biased.

"You wouldn't see her when she came to the hospital. Her face was streaked with tears, she couldn't sit down, and she wouldn't talk to anyone. She kept wringing her hands, and her eyes were red rimmed. Out of the people in the waiting room, no one look as scared as Tallulah. She wasn't gossiping with the others about what caused the wreck or whispering about how Haegan's body looked. Or how they had to cut him from the car. She was quiet. Her eyes on the door. Waiting on any word about you. And when I sent her home, all she said was that she loved you. Because of what I saw, I can tell you I don't think she did shit with Dace. I don't know why you're pissed at her, but that girl ain't got a selfish, mean bone in her body."

He was my cousin. He'd never tell a soul. He wouldn't hurt her with the truth. I waited until the bell rang and the hallway was clear, then I turned to him. "That day. The day of the accident. I saw them. Tallulah and Dace. Haegan was with me. It's why I smoked the fucking weed. I was hurting. Heartbroken. She kissed him then."

Ryker listened. He didn't respond right away. I knew he was thinking it over. Just like I knew he'd never share this with anyone. Finally he looked at me. "I didn't see what you did. I wasn't there. But I'm gonna ask you one thing. Are you sure you saw it all? Did you stay and watch what happened after? Did she appear to be enjoying it? Did she want it?"

I opened my mouth to say yes and stopped. Because I didn't know. I hadn't seen anything after the kiss. I'd been fucking destroyed. I'd left.

"I don't . . . I left. . . ."

Ryker raised both eyebrows. "Then just maybe you should find out what happened next. That is, if you're still thinking about her. If the idea of her being run out of school bothers you. If not, then let it go. Move on. There are a lot of Blakelys out there to choose from."

He didn't stand there and wait for my answer. He left. He didn't need my response.

He expected me to make the right decision. For the first time since I'd seen the kiss, I began to doubt it. With that came a sickening feeling in my gut.

The Best Is Yet to Come for You,
Sweetheart
CHAPTER 47

TALLULAH

It was Wednesday when Brett texted me the first time. I'd been in my house since I got home Monday. Figuring out the virtual school process. It had kept me busy, and I had only thought about it all when I lay down at night. When my room was quiet and I was alone. I cried then. Quietly, so my mother wouldn't hear. I didn't want her worrying any more than she already did.

She wanted a normal high school experience for me. I wasn't going to have that. After my brief dip into it, I decided I didn't want it. Graduation and college were my future. They'd be different. I'd go somewhere far away from this place.

Brett's text said, Dinner Friday night and a movie?

I read it three times before thinking it over. This was a date. I'd tried that already. It hadn't ended well. I didn't want to get hurt again. But then what were the chances of that? Brett was nice, but he wasn't Nash. I didn't feel giddy when he was near me. He didn't make my heart race, and I had no thoughts of him unless I was speaking to him.

It wasn't possible to get hurt by him. He didn't have a piece of me. I didn't respond, though. I was too busy holding the phone, thinking it through.

Then he sent another text as I stared down at it.

They made an announcement today. Haswell said that Dace admitted to making advances to you. That you did nothing wrong and were taken advantage of. Those talking about you and accusing you will stop. If it is brought to his attention, the student doing so will be suspended. He went on to talk about the no bullying code. Once he was done, all the talk was about how they didn't think you were like that anyway.

I read the text several times.

I even wondered if I had read it incorrectly. Or if this was a dream.

Another text lit up my screen. It was Nash.

Are you home? We need to talk.

That text was like a jab directly in my chest. Nash was texting me. He'd heard the announcement and was now wanting to talk. He'd hurt me. Pushed me away for no reason. Then, when I needed him the most, he abandoned me. Left me alone to face it all by myself.

I replied to Nash's text:

No thanks.

Then I turned my phone off. I didn't want to read any more. I wasn't ready to date Brett, either. That one text from Nash had ripped me open again. Made me bleed. I curled into a ball and focused on long, deep breaths. That lasted all of five seconds, and then the tears came.

Crying didn't make it go away. It didn't fix the past, but it was all I could do.

A knock on my bedroom door right before my mother opened it wasn't enough of a warning to dry my tears and clean up my face. Instead, she found me there, falling apart. I didn't want her to worry. I didn't want her to know how much I was hurting. But she'd caught me. I turned over to look at her, and the tears came harder. My body shook with each sob, and I couldn't make it stop if I'd wanted to.

My mother's arms were around me immediately as she lay down beside me on the bed. She didn't ask me why I was crying or try to make me stop. She just held me tightly in her arms while I got it all out. The pain I'd been hiding. I had wanted to fit in and be a part of something. To have friends. To have Nash. But now all that seemed stupid to me. It hadn't brought me anything but heartache. I had been fine the way I was before.

I'm not sure how long I cried or how long we lay there after the sobs slowed to small sniffles. But when I finally calmed down, it did feel better. My chest was lighter. The pain wasn't gone, but crying had released something. I don't know—maybe I'd been trying to be tough for so long I just needed to be weak for once. Let it go. Not put so much pressure on myself.

My mom kissed my forehead. "This has been awful, but it will soon pass. I promise it isn't forever. High school isn't the end. It's just a stepping stone. You've learned a lot about life these past few years. College will be easier on you because you didn't live a fantasy in high school. The best is yet to come for you, sweetheart."

I know she believed everything she said. I wanted to believe her, but I was scared to believe in anything now. It was my senior year, and I was finishing it with homeschool. I would get to graduate like the others, but they'd all go to parties and on trips together. They'd have memories to share, and they'd make promises to be friends forever. All the stuff I'd read in books and seen in movies. But me, no one would have a memory with me. I wouldn't have a party or be invited to one. I'd simply walk, get my diploma, and this would be over.

"I got a call from Officer Mike. He wants to know if we want to press charges. He said that Mr. Dace confessed to it all. Which we already knew. I don't want to make this decision for you. I want it to be yours. I will stand behind whatever you want to do."

I didn't much care about what happened to Mr. Dace. But I did care about his daughter. She'd lost a father in this. Her family would be broken now. Her father would be labeled something she wouldn't understand. She was just a baby. It seemed so unfair.

"No. It's over. Let it go."

Mom nodded. "I figured you'd say that. But I am going to file a restraining order for your protection. If his wife thinks he could try to come see you, then I think it is wise."

I shrugged. I didn't think I'd see Mr. Dace again. But if it made her feel better, then that was okay with me. "Do you think his daughter will be okay? I mean, she had a dad, and now she's losing him. I think it would be easier to have never had one at all."

My mom squeezed me tightly. "I don't think she had a very good father. He wasn't thinking about her when he made the decisions he did. In her case it is better to have him out of her life now rather than later. He needs help."

I hoped she was right.

"Are they going to leave town? Charlotte and her daughter?"

"I don't know. She didn't say," Mom replied.

"I think starting a new life away from the memories of her father would be easier."

Mom nodded. "You're probably right."

We lay there silently, both staring at the ceiling for several minutes. My thoughts were on Mr. Dace's little girl and wife. Where they would go and how their life would be now. I realized that, yes, my world had been changed with his choices, but theirs had been destroyed. They'd have to build again. It was like Momma always told me. Somewhere someone else is having a worse day than you. Be thankful for what you have. I had a mother who loved me. A home with oddly painted ceilings, that always smelled like a bakery. I was healthy. I would go to college next year. My life wasn't so bad. I would be okay.

I Didn't Want Her to Be My Past

CHAPTER 48

NASH

Tonight would be my first night on the field coaching. I'd been to every practice this week. I'd worked out with the team. This all should have made me feel good. Hell, I should have been excited. Ready for this.

But there was Tallulah. And I couldn't think about anything else. She wasn't responding to my texts. After her first "no thanks" she'd been silent. I checked my phone again, hoping my last text I had finally sent this morning would get a response. So far nothing.

Telling her in a text message that I'd seen her kiss Dace the day of the accident wasn't what I wanted to do, but when I called her phone, it went directly to voice mail. She wasn't talking to me. She'd cut herself off completely. Brett had been talking to Hannah in the hallway earlier this morning, which made me think she'd stopped talking to him, too.

I didn't want to think of Tallulah alone, closed off from life. She had so much to give. She was fun and kind. She was smart, and she wanted to be social. She'd finally had her chance to get that this year, and so quickly it had been shut down. But that fucking kiss. I needed to hear her explanation of it. No matter what Dace had confessed to, I saw her kiss him. I was there. That didn't change.

"You good?" Asa asked, stopping beside my locker.

"Yeah, why?" I replied, taking out my notebook and closing the door.

"Oh, I don't know. Because you were standing here staring blankly into your locker like you were a million miles away?"

"I was just thinking."

He laughed "Yeah, I gathered that much."

Glancing at the hallway full of people hurrying to their classes, I suddenly felt more out of place than ever. No amount of football made that better. It wasn't making me happy. One thing had made me happy since my accident. Tallulah. Since that fucking kiss I'd been miserable. I didn't want to feel this way. I was tired of it . . . and I missed her. I missed her so damn much.

She didn't want to talk to me. She didn't care about explaining the kiss I saw. She was shutting me out. Done. Which scared me because I couldn't let her go.

"I love her," I said the words aloud. Admitted them to myself and Asa. I had to tell someone. Come clean. Stop pretending she had hurt me and I was done. Because no matter how badly she'd broken me, I still loved her.

"No shit," Asa replied, amused.

I turned my head to look at him. "What?"

He shrugged. "You said you loved her. I said no shit. That's been obvious since the beginning. It's why I backed off. I liked her. She's smoking hot. But I didn't feel the way you obviously did. There was a look in your eyes that said it was more to you. She was more to you."

"Really?" I asked, amazed that Asa had noticed all this and it had taken me this long to admit it to myself.

"Yeah, man. Really. My question is why did you turn on her?"

"Because I thought she'd lied to me."

Asa nodded. "Had she?"

I didn't know. Not really. "I'm not sure."

Asa frowned. "You're not sure?" His tone sounded like I was an idiot.

"Yeah, I'm not sure."

With a shake of his head he nodded toward the door.

"Then you should go find out. You're miserable. She left school. Why are you just letting it continue to fall apart? Soon you'll be past the point of no return, and she will be your past."

I didn't want her to be my past. That wasn't even acceptable. We had just begun. Dace had screwed with it. But I missed her. The nightmares that still haunted me at night. Haegan's lifeless face there in my dreams. I had no one to talk to about them. I didn't want to talk to anyone else. Just her. She'd listen. She'd be there. She was who I wanted.

"I gotta go," I told him, and headed for the exit.

"That's my boy!" he called out just before I shoved the door open and broke into a run—or the best I could do with my limp. The anxiety began to mount as the fear that I'd waited too long built. She might not be able to forgive me. The kiss I'd seen now seemed pointless compared to never seeing Tallulah again. Never sitting with her and watching her smile. Never holding her against me. Never feeling her hand firmly in mine.

Her parking spot remained empty, and I hated seeing that. I hadn't realized how I depended on seeing her car there every day until it was gone. I drove faster than I had in a while. I didn't speed because I wanted to make it there alive. That fear was never going to go away.

When I arrived at her house, I pulled into the driveway

behind her car. I didn't know just yet what I was going to say or if I could even get her to open her door. But I had to try. If she didn't come to the door, I'd find another way. But I wasn't leaving here until we'd talked. Until I'd seen her. Until I told her I loved her.

I rang the doorbell and waited. No answer. I knocked. Waited. Nothing. I tried the doorbell again. I pulled my phone out and called her. Got her voice mail immediately. This went on for a good five minutes. Finally I had to come up with another plan. She knew I was out here. She could see my Escalade from any window in her house.

Stepping back, I looked up at her bedroom window and saw the curtain move a little. She was watching. She was here. I tried the doorbell again. Then I stepped back farther, cupped my hands around my mouth, and shouted, "PLEASE, TALLULAH! TALK TO ME! I'M NOT LEAVING UNTIL YOU DO!"

No movement. I waited and looked at the door to see if she'd decided to come on down. But after plenty of time, nothing happened. I was going in. I tried the door and it was locked. So I started working my way around the house, trying each window. Each one was firmly shut and locked. What was wrong with these people? Did they never open their windows?

It took five windows with no luck before I made

it around to the back of her house. The back porch was painted like a blue sky with a rainbow across it. Smiling, I shook my head. Her mom was an interesting person. I went onto the porch and tried the door not expecting it to open . . . when it did. I paused and slowly pushed it open. Glancing around, I saw I was in the kitchen. Chocolate chip cookies were on a plate beside the oven. A red cake was displayed on a stand in the middle of the table. And it smelled like heaven in here. I closed the door quietly behind me.

There was a slight chance—okay a good chance—that Tallulah would call the cops on me. I honestly didn't give a shit. I needed to talk to her. Maybe I could say all I needed before they showed up to cuff me and book me.

I tried to walk as softly as I could. As soon as she knew I was in her house, my time would begin ticking. I was almost to the bottom of the stairs when she rounded the corner, then screamed as her eyes went wide.

Her scream died quickly as she realized it was me standing in her house. She covered her mouth, her eyes wide as she stared at me as if I were insane. Maybe I was. I felt like it. I'd never been desperate enough to break into someone's house.

"I need to say something. Please listen to me," I started.

Tallulah had regained her composure and pointed to the front door. "Get out!"

"Just let me—"

"GET OUT!"

"Tallulah, please, just—"

"I SAID TO GET OUT!"

"Did you get my last text?"

"GET OUT!"

"I sent it this morning—"

"GET OUT!"

She made a move toward me now. Both her hands landed on my chest, and she shoved me backward. "I SAID TO GET OUT OF MY HOUSE!"

I'd never seen her angry. Not like this. Her eyes wild with all kinds of emotions. The pain was there, though. She was hiding it the best she could, but I had looked into those eyes enough to know what I saw.

"LEAVE." She shoved me back again. This time harder. "MY HOUSE!"

I let her push me. I stumbled back with each shove to my chest. She needed this. Her eyes began to turn glassy. I couldn't take this anymore. I didn't give a fuck if she'd kissed the teacher. It was forgiven. I was over it. I would never be able to get over losing her.

"I love you," I said simply, staring into her eyes, hoping she could see past her pain and anger.

She pushed me again, but this time a sob escaped her. "No! You don't!"

I reached for her then. My hands gently wrapping around her arms. "Yes. I do. I love you. I miss you."

She started to shove me again and dropped her hands back down, then began to cry. Her shoulders shaking. My heart broke over and over again with each sound. I hated this. Moving in, I pulled her into my arms and held her as she cried. I had done this to her. Or I'd at least been a part of it. She'd needed me and I'd left her. Turned against her like everyone else.

"I don't deserve your forgiveness. But I'm begging you for it. I love you, Tallulah. I was hurt, blindsided, and then I saw my friend die. It messed with me. I should have talked to you about it. Not shut you out."

She sniffled and tilted her head back to look at me. "What did I do that blindsided you?"

I'd texted her. "My text?"

She shook her head. "My phone has been off for almost a week."

So she'd seen nothing. She didn't know why I'd closed her out. And she was still letting me hold me right now. That was humbling. It also gave me hope.

"I saw you kiss Dace."

Love Isn't Supposed to Turn
on You So Easily
CHAPTER 49

TALLULAH

"What?" I was stunned. Out of all the things he was going to say, that wasn't what I had imagined.

"The day of the accident. I saw you. Haegan was with me. I was coming to find you. Talk after our argument at lunch. And I saw you kiss Dace. But I don't care. Not anymore. I just want you. I want to be with you. I love you."

I shook my head and backed up. "You saw *me* kiss Mr. Dace?" I asked to clarify. Because I had never kissed Mr. Dace. I'd been attacked by the man. What Nash was describing never happened.

"I came to the room, Tallulah. I saw him lean in and kiss you. So, technically, I guess he kissed you."

I waited for more, but he said nothing. "Did you see what happened next? Where were you when I shoved him off me in complete shock? Or when I ran from the room and he followed me into the women's restroom? Did you see when he told me he loved me? Were you watching when I begged him to leave me alone?"

His expression said it all. He'd seen nothing but the kiss. He had believed the worst. He hadn't trusted me. And when I needed him most, he wasn't there. When I needed him, he had pushed me away.

"Shit, Tallulah," he whispered. "God, I am so sorry. I didn't know. I saw the kiss. I couldn't watch it. I was hurt. I left. I didn't know."

"And I didn't know why you shut me out. I have never been as scared as I was when I stood for hours on the street, watching, waiting for anything. Someone to tell me you were alive. That you were okay. All I wanted to do was see you, touch you. Know you were breathing. But you sent me away without a word."

He sighed and ran his hand over his face. "I'm an idiot."

"You say you love me, Nash. But I can't be sure I believe that. Love isn't supposed to turn on you so easily. Love is supposed to be stronger. Isn't it?"

We stood there silently staring at each other. I never expected to hear Nash Lee tell me he loved me. He'd broken into my house to do it. Even when I had shut him out every way I could. But forgiving him. Forgetting what he did, that made me vulnerable.

"I messed up. I can't apologize enough. If you can't forgive me, if you can't love me, please . . . don't shut me out. I can't lose you completely. If all I can have is your friendship, then I'll take it. Just to see you smile at me. To be close to you. If I can have that . . . if it's all I can have, I will take it."

I stood there, unable to respond to that. Was he serious? Was that what real love was? To take whatever you could get, even if it hurt you daily? Did I love him that much?

I did.

Losing him had cracked me, then crushed me. I missed him. Just this. Being near him gave me a peace. It shouldn't. We were throwing it all out there. How we felt. The lies. The truths. The hurt. And still in this moment I had a feeling of being whole. Because he was with me. He was here.

"I had decided it was easier to not know love or experience it than to have it and lose it. Knowing what you lost is more painful than not knowing what you've never had. But . . . I think I was wrong." I sighed and wiped away the tears still on my face before continuing. "I think that knowing love, having the experience, feeling the joy of it, is something everyone should have in life. It's part of life. It's what ultimately drives us. We do everything because of love. Knowing how it felt to love you, to be with you, it was there even when I was in a dark place. The memory helped. As much as it hurt, it also got me through."

Nash's expression was tense. Almost nervous. Unsure. "Does that mean you're good with just having the memory? Or do I have a chance? Because I really want a chance, Tallulah. More than I've wanted anything in my life. I can stand here and honestly tell you that if I was given a choice right now between my leg being completely healed and my future at football restored, or having your forgiveness and a chance to have your love. I'd choose you. I swear it."

It was hard to believe that. But his face was so sincere. His eyes now held unshed tears. He'd been hurting too. Differently than me, but he'd been alone in his own way. Fitting in at school, having friends, it didn't fix everything. We all were alone at some point, even in a crowded room.

"More than football?" I was smiling when I asked.

A slow smile touched his face. "I swear."

Forgiveness is a choice. It's taking a chance. It's making yourself vulnerable. But it's what you have to do if you want to live a full life. Hiding from it all isn't living. I know. I'd tried it many times. Not once had I been happy hiding from it. Forgetting is harder. It's letting go of the armor you put in place. It's opening yourself back up. It's the only way to truly be happy.

"I've loved you most of my life," I admitted to him. "For most of it I loved you from afar. I didn't really know you. But once I got the chance, I quickly fell in love. It was impossible not to."

He took a step toward me. Cautiously. "Does this mean we aren't going to just be friends? That I have another chance?" His tone hopeful and achingly sweet.

"Did you actually think we could just be friends?" I asked him, amused.

He shrugged. "No. Not really. But I was grabbing at anything I could. If you only wanted to be my friend, I would have taken it. I'd have scowled at anyone who got close to you. Probably caused problems, made you yell at me." He was grinning now and stepping closer. "I'd also end up trying to kiss you, and you would slap me in the face."

Our chests were touching now. My thighs brushed against his. I could smell the mint from his gum as his breath mingled with mine. Being close to him like this made my knees weak. I imagined it always would. Nothing could change that.

"I don't think I would slap you." My words came out in a whisper as my gaze dropped to his lips. He had really good lips, especially for a guy.

"No?" he asked as his palm touched my back and he pressed me closer. His mouth was almost on mine.

"Definitely not." My voice trembled, and then his lips touched mine.

We were both different now. We'd gone through a lot in a short amount of time. But one thing was the same. This was where we belonged. We'd found our perfect fit in an unlikely situation.

Acknowledgments

The first BIG thank you goes to my daughter Annabelle. She answered countless questions about vloggers, gave me vlogs to watch, filled my head full of a world I didn't realize existed. I was stuck on the story line. In the car one day I mentioned it. Annabelle said, "Put a vlogger in there. It'll make it interesting." I went home and did just that. She saved the day . . . or the writer's block.

My editor, Jennifer Ung. She helped me mold this story into what it has become. I am so very proud of it and thankful to have her on my team. Also I want to mention Mara Anastas, Jodie Hockensmith, Caitlin Sweeny, and the rest of the Simon Pulse team for all their hard work in getting my books out there.

My agent, Jane Dystel, always has my back, and I can trust she'll support my decisions. Having an agent is like a marriage. I'm thankful I have the best.

When I started writing, I never imagined having a group of readers come together for the sole purpose of supporting me. Abbi's Army, led by Danielle Lagasse and Vicci Kaighan, humbles me and gives me a place of refuge. When I need my spirits lifted, these ladies are there. I love every one of you.

Last but certainly not least: my family. Without their

support I wouldn't be here. My kids, who understand my deadlines and help around the house. My parents, who have supported me all along. Even when I decided to write steamier stuff. My friends, who don't hate me because I can't because my writing is taking over. They are my ultimate support group, and I love them dearly.

Britt Sullivan for listening to me rant, helping me work through story lines, and understanding how moody I can be when writing a book. He's not only a wonderful father but a man that I am thankful to have by my side.

My readers. I never expected to have so many of you. Thank you for reading my books. For loving them and telling others about them. Without you I wouldn't be here. It's that simple.